Swimming with
& other stories

JEREMY WORMAN

INDEPENDENT INNOVATIVE INTERNATIONAL

Published by Cinnamon Press,
Meirion House,
Tanygrisiau,
Blaenau Ffestiniog,
Gwynedd
LL41 3SU
www.cinnamonpress.com

ISBN 978-1-909077-22-5
British Library Cataloguing in Publication Data. A CIP record for
this book can be obtained from the British Library.

Designed and typeset in Garamond by Cinnamon Press. Cover design by Jan Fortune, from original art work, 'Retro Home View of
Pool' by Diana Rich, agency Dreamstime © Diana Rich

Cinnamon Press is represented by Inpress
and by the Welsh Books Council in Wales.

Printed in Poland

Acknowledgements

I would like to thank Barbara Hardy, Jan Fortune, Christopher Sinclair-Stevenson and all the teachers and students connected to the MA in Creative and Life Writing at Goldsmiths, University of London, whose support made this book possible.

Contents

Places

London

And by came an Angel who had a bright key,
And he open'd the coffins & set them all free;
Then down a green plain leaping, laughing, they run,
And wash in a river, and shine in the Sun.

William Blake, 'The Chimney Sweeper',

from *Songs of Innocence* (1789)

For Alan Ross

1922-2001,

Editor of *The London Magazine* 1961-2001

Swimming with Diana Dors

Places

Boys and the Berlin Wall

The black shiny Humber Hawk arrived to collect my cousin Captain David Lister from his army quarters. David walked out, his brown shoes as polished as the car's bodywork. I was in the front garden with my friend John.

'Don't go to the border, boys, and be back for the final.'

'Might cross over to East Berlin for a coffee,' I replied.

'Don't be so damn silly, Richard.'

The driver opened the rear door and saluted. David tapped the roof with his swagger stick; I'm sure he thought he was a brigadier. 'And don't wear that bloody flowery shirt to curry night at the mess tomorrow. They'll think you're a queer.' He got in and opened the window. 'You have a tie?'

'I was planning to wear my ban-the-bomb tee-shirt, actually.'

'No wonder your father is worried about you.'

The car sped off.

'Fascist bastard,' I mumbled.

John had retreated into the shadows.

'Sorry about that,' I said.

'Why are you always so political?'

'He's so annoying. Come on, let's go.'

1966 could be our year to win the World Cup, I thought, but I hope Jimmy Greaves would be playing, as he was better than Roger Hunt. I was trying to be enthusiastic about football to make my mother less unhappy with me for hating sport. We soon reached the track at the edge of the army officers' quarters where the sandy ground blew up a cloud from our plimsolls. High fir trees sliced the sun into strips. I tied my loose laces.

'This way,' John said and I followed him.

John was tall with curly blond hair and a pale elfin face that was mischievous and happy when he was away from adults. He didn't go to public school in England, unlike most of the officers' children. At the tree with the secret mark he dug down and found his Thermos flask of orange juice, the packet of custard creams and two bars of Fry's milk chocolate we had bought the day before at Toc H.

'Let's get as close as we can to the barbed wire today,' he said.

'Definitely.'

We had a drink and ate half the biscuits.

> 'Three German officers crossed the Rhine
> Parlez-vous
> Three German officers crossed the Rhine
> To fuck the women and drink the wine
> Hinky-dinky parlez-vous.'

John knew more verses than anyone. I'd probably learn them all before Mother and I returned to England. Really, it was a bit tedious but I could recite them to the rugger buggers back at school and perhaps they would stop calling me 'Richard-the-red-under-the-bed'. We buried our supplies again and carried on.

Once this forest would have stretched as far as Russia and there was no Berlin Wall. John hated the 'Ruskies' and I had tried to say it's more complicated but we quarrelled. Fir trees grew thick. You had to watch out for grass snakes. Using a map and compass we avoided the main paths and soon the watchtowers of the Vopos, the East German guards, came into sight. We spread-eagled in long grass and John looked at the two grey towers through his binoculars. 'Lots of activity today,' he said and handed them to me. I was going to write something about the divided city of Berlin for the school magazine. I liked the idea of being a political journalist.

I got up and stood behind a chestnut tree, peered through a slit in the foliage and adjusted the focus as I scanned the border fence. Last week David had taken my mother and me in an army car to East Berlin. He and the driver were in uniform. It was a sunny day but the other side of Checkpoint Charlie became a black-and-white-world, no, a grey world: clothes and faces were grey; cars were ugly and smelly. At the Soviet War Memorial in Treptower Park people huddled round us and a young girl offered mother a posy of flowers. Two men in dark suits ran across the road and held up badges to the small crowd, who dispersed like ants. 'Stasi,' David whispered. My mother asked in German, 'May I use my camera? I was here before the war.' One of the men bowed mockingly but let her take one photograph. On the far pavement soldiers in ceremonial uniform did a high-stepping march. We watched from the car for a while, then drove back and I saw that mother was crying. 'Did 80,000 Russians die in the Battle of Berlin for this?' I handed her my handkerchief. 'It's so changed, I hardly recognised anything....'

John leant against the tree and ate chocolate: 'The communists would be all over us if we let them.'

Alsatians ran along a track beneath the towers. 'Schnell, Schnell!' A voice shouted and a Vopo turned in our direction and sunlight slashed the lens of his binoculars. A rifle bullet ricocheted. 'He shot at me!' I said.

'Get down.'

We slithered thirty yards to the right, and the ferns were camouflage. Behind us the dogs' barks became raucous.

'Of course they're not firing at us,' John said.

Crows squawked. I peeped round the wide trunk of an alder tree, at the watchtower on the eastern edge, before the border fence turned a corner. Two Vopos from the tower shot at the top of a pine, and heavy cones dropped near us. They laughed and shouted in our direction. We lay flat on our bellies.

'They're trying to scare us,' I said.

We stayed still for a while and then looked. The Alsatians were pacing along a concrete strip where the barbed wire had been peeled back. On the tower, a Vopo cupped his hands round a cigarette as his colleague lit it.

'Run, Run!' John screamed, and we didn't stop for ages. In a clearing we panted and sat with our backs against a tree.

'That was no man's land; the dogs shouldn't have been allowed there.'

'Don't mention this to anyone.' John put his shaking hand to his lips.

'We must.'

'If British army officers' children get caught in an incident it looks bad.'

'They're bullies.'

'Bad for my father. Please.'

'Okay.'

The birds were singing, the sun was warm, the air fresh with pine — and those guards could get away with frightening us.

'Communists are evil bastards, but we've got freedom,' John said.

I lay down. The sky was very blue and the creaky trees swayed. What Obolensky had said to me at school came into my mind: he would have been a prince before the revolution and his ancient grandmother told him, she was certain, that in a secret corner of Russia there was a green forest where some of her old friends were still living. It sounded like a mad old dame, but Obo showed me two letters from one of these aristocrats, posted last year in Leningrad.

'We'd better get back,' John said.

'Yes.'

I suppose it was a fairytale. We were lucky to be free, that was true. After leaving the forest John went straight

16

home. I rang the bell of my cousin's house. Mother opened the door; the porch was painted a uniform white like all the other little houses for officers with wives and children, but David was always lucky and had a house to himself.

'Such a successful shopping trip to the Kurfürstendamm! German sausages and pumpernickel are wonderful.' She hugged me. 'Daddy and I don't want to quarrel with you, but you're so argumentative these days.'

'Lot to argue about.'

'All that money to send you to a good school, and your father having to do extra tonsil operations this week at that private clinic — and you have these awful ideas. I know it's just a phase.'

'Like capitalism.'

'Do you always have to be so clever?' She stamped on the heel of her brown lace-up shoe.

'Sorry.'

I followed her in to the bare white sitting room. She picked up a silver-framed photograph from the side table. 'I was close to my sister Barbara and when she died David was left without a mother — he was only twelve — and a father who was loving but too wrapped up in his work. I did my best to keep in touch with David. He has done very well. The army suits him.'

'I know, Ma, I've tried, but he's always the tough guy, who always has to be right — and he's always picking on me.'

'It's a defence, and don't spoil things, only two more days.'

'I'll do my best.'

She kissed her sister's photograph and put it back.

'Go and have a shower then, Comrade Son.'

Upstairs, as I closed the bathroom door, I heard David in the hallway: 'How's my favourite aunt. May I get you anything?' His voice was like a grenade and I turned the shower to full. I dressed quickly, unlocked the door, and found David standing in front of the small mirror on the landing. His tortoiseshell comb made a perfect parting in his dark hair as he stared at my reflection. 'I know a very good barber.'

'I only know very bad ones and therefore avoid them.'

He turned. 'We've got to be at Retread's for 3pm as he's having a bash for the World Cup.' His breath was hot on my face. 'Trust you didn't go to the border?'

'Of course not.' I kept my eyes on his.

I went downstairs. Mother was standing by the window in the sitting room. 'It's always cold in here, isn't it?'

'What does "Retread" mean, Ma?'

'It's what they call John's father, Major Timms, because he came up through the ranks.'

'That's horrible.'

David stood at the door and tapped his watch. 'Sure you won't come, favourite aunt?' The creases in his cavalry twill trousers were as sharp as knives when he bent down and kissed Ma on the head.

'No, I want to try that German recipe for pork casserole. You two get off, but I'll be thinking about the English team.'

'That'll do the trick. Bye, Ma.'

Major Timms opened the door. 'Come in, you two, come in.' He patted my shoulder. 'John has enjoyed having you around this week.'

He was tall with grey hairs flecked through the black. In the sitting room a few other officers chatted, all younger than the major. David helped himself to a bottle of German lager.

'How's the brigadier's bum boy then?' a chubby blond man with a red face slapped his arm.

'Don't be rude, Tubby, we are in the house of a major,' David replied.

'Pity we're not watching a proper game of rugby,' Tubby said.

Major Timms stood at the kitchen door. 'Football is even more skilful than rugby in its way,' he said, 'especially Swansea Town — and I don't have anything to learn about rugby from an Englishman. We won 14-3 at Cardiff Arms Park last time, if you recall.'

They mumbled something. David was the brigadier's aide-de-camp and it seemed to impress people. He turned up the television volume, 'It's only in kraut talk, but the English team look fit.'

'Come on, young Richard, let me get you a drink,' Major Timms said.

'Coke, please.'

At Wembley the players lined up for the national anthems. Jimmy Greaves wasn't playing. Anyway, I was going to like football for the next hour and a half because I was supporting Major Timms. 'May I help, Mrs Timms?' I called out and went in to the kitchen.

'We're doing very well, thank you, Richard.' Her thick arms shaped the top layer of pastry on the sausage rolls. 'We baked lovely cakes when I was a girl in Swansea.' She smiled and popped thcm in the oven. John tipped peanuts into a bowl but didn't look up. The major took out a bottle of Johnny Walker from the top cupboard.

'Don't miss your football,' she said.

John and I followed Major Timms into the sitting room. David had the best chair; Richard and I sat on stools.

'More lager, gentlemen?' The major held up two bottles in each hand and they took one each.

'Up the Welsh,' Tubby said as he took his.

The young officers laughed loudly at a dirty joke about two German nuns. The teams stood still for the national anthems.

'Zieg Heil!' Tubby gave a Nazi salute which made them laugh.

The match began. 'Come on England!' I raised my arm. The major sat on a hard chair at the table of snacks and poured himself another whisky. We kept possession well, then lost it, brilliant pass to Helmut Haller – 1-nil in the twelfth minute. Hurst equalised soon after. Alan Ball and Martin Peters were elegant in midfield but Beckenbauer's passes were deadly. Their central defenders, Willi Schulz and Wolfgang Weber, snuffed out the English forwards, and the fizzing runs of Lothar Emmerich put our right back George Cohen under pressure. Half time: 1-1.

'That is wonderful football,' Major Timms stood up and clapped. He reached behind the vase of lilacs for the whisky.

I opened the kitchen door; Mrs Timms came in holding up a big white china plate of sausage rolls, and handed them round. Then she and John took out the empty bottles.

'Gosh, these are good,' Tubby whispered, 'must have learnt to cook when she was in service.'

'Bobby Moore has nice legs for his age,' David said.

Tubby's hand shook from his cackling, and lager spilt on the carpet.

After seventy-six minutes, still 1-1. Alan Ball took a corner, Peters scored after a deflection from Hurst. David and the other young officers flicked peanuts and whooped. Major Timms was on the edge of his seat. The Germans equalised – it went into extra time – and then Hurst scored! Just before the whistle he scored again. Final score: England 4, Germany 2. We'd won the World Cup and the room exploded with cheers. 'Almost as good as rugby,' Tubby sprayed all the peanuts into the air.

'Now that's enough!' Major Timms stood up and pushed the back of Tubby's neck, making Tubby drop his glass, which broke against the mantelpiece. 'My dear fellow officers, isn't it time you public school men learnt some manners; we had more courtesy in my Port Talbot secondary modern. Now pick up every one – and the glass.'

Mrs Timms rushed in. 'Only a bit of fun, love.' She squeezed her husband's broad shoulders. He walked out with the Johnny Walker.

I went upstairs to the lavatory but stood for a moment on the landing as David talked in the hallway to Tubby: 'Better calm down. Nothing like a Royal Army Ordnance Corps major when he's roused.'

As I came out, David was standing there.

'Why don't you leave him alone, you bastard,' I said.

He shoved me against the wall. 'You're going to be a communist when you grow up, aren't you?'

'At least I will grow up. Why not hit me? Then they'll know what you're really like.'

'You've had it easy, and in a few years no doubt you'll be at university, one of those lefties who does nothing for their country.' He twisted my wrist. 'How does that feel?'

'Why don't you admit you miss your mother?'

'Fucking little shit.' He jerked up my elbow.

'Maybe there are no good teams, just bullies on both sides − let go!'

He dropped my arm. I put my head close and his lips quivered. He went downstairs. Shooting pains wound up my back, and my arm was limp. I locked the bathroom door, shook, cried, and rinsed my face in cold water. I breathed slowly and after a few minutes felt well enough to go down.

In the kitchen I said goodbye to Mrs Timms and John, who kept his eyes on the washing up. Major Timms lit a Woodbine on the back doorstep.

'Don't go so soon, Richard. We were hoping you'd stay for supper.'

'Thank you, but my mother is cooking a special meal.'

'Quite understand.' He stood up and shook my hand. 'Your hair's a bit long, and I noticed the flowery shirt, but I could make a bloody good officer out of you.'

'Well, thank you very much.' I looked away. 'Goodbye.'

I ran into the sunlight. John caught me up and said he would teach me more verses from 'Mademoiselle from Armentières'.

'I've learnt enough, but thanks. I'll see you before we leave. Bye.'

I went in to the forest. It was darker now and there was no one around. I began to sob and I didn't stop running till I reached the border. New barbed wire had been rolled out, the silver tips glinting.

Holy Russia

Rasputin's eyes cover me like silk sheets. I drown in his strange smell; he is more with us than when he was alive.

'Anastasia! Anastasia! Anastasia!' If I call my name his eyes peel off me.

A soldier bangs open the door with his rifle butt. Mama, sitting closest to the door, turns.

'Who was Rasputin's whore then!'

His vodka-and-garlic sausage smell is foul in the cold air. When he leaves he bows mockingly, a piece of gristle caught in his beard. Outside, other soldiers stamp their feet. Wild beasts. Then a so-called captain comes in, filthy uniform, unshaven. 'The commandant is coming to see you later, scum.' He punches his fist in the air.

Will we live in the Winter Palace again? I see a glass palace stoned by a mob. At least we are together once more as a family, and blessed to have with us a few of our closest helpers, including Dr Botkin, and Sydney Gibbes, our tutor. I loved the winters at Tsarsko Selo when we would toboggan through the trees and the air was pure, the sky blue. Now I only smell grease, oil, rotting food and soldiers.

Supper time. Papa sits upright at the top of the table and puts his hand to his ear, listening to the soldiers' receding footsteps. From under the table he draws out a bottle of wine like a conjurer. It is our last bottle of the six, Chateau Yquem 1906, smuggled in, a gift from a cousin in England. Papa pours a little into each of our smeared glasses: Mama, Olga, Tatiana, Marie, me, Dr Botkin and Sydney Gibbes. I write down their names. I write them again and again. Now I am certain they will be here forever, that all will be well.

Papa says: 'Put your diary down, Anastasia. You're becoming a bookworm. When we live in England I shall have to send you to Girton.'

'That says something for my teaching, sir!' Mr Gibbes suggests. Everyone laughs, and our happiness moves outwards, keeping us forever safe in the circle of Our Mother.

Two days ago Father Storozhev celebrated mass with us and I tried to think of Our Mother, but I saw rats scuttling. The biggest spoke: 'Eat the Tzar's children, eat them.' I take wine to Alexei who is sitting up in his little bed in the corner. He holds the glass in both hands like a little child.

Dr Botkin looks at Papa: 'To the Tzar of all the Russias!' When Papa looks up Dr Botkin lowers his eyes.

Papa toasts Alexei. 'To the next Tzar of all the Russias!'

Alexei salutes.

Tatiana pretends to savour her herring: 'Gorgeous salmon this year!'

I begin to watch us all as if I am no longer here.

The black woods are tipped with ice.

From the dark their brooding eyes on us.

The windows are boarded up. Soldiers' boots crack on the gravel, their rifles shoot into the air, and they smash empty vodka bottles. Some urinate through holes in the walls of our flimsy building, making it smell like a stable.

Yesterday, when we exercised in the yard, they sang a revolutionary song. Their eyes were black and opaque, as if they could not see an outside world. One of the Letts mercenaries, his face purple-red from a wound, lifted up Tatiana's skirt: 'Ever had a good man up there!'

Three soldiers spun her round, and gestured with their crotches. She slipped and fell on her back. Mama stood over her and said calmly to the young soldier with the purple-red face: 'I see your foot is wounded too. Give me bandages and I shall dress it for you.'

Another soldier smirked, 'Get your wound dressed by the Tsarina and Rasputin will guarantee you eternal life!' They heckled, but someone handed Mama a bottle of iodine, dressings and a bowl of water.

She bent down and undid the young soldier's boot, cleaned his wound, a great mass of pus. The heckling stopped. Mama spoke a prayer to the Holy Mother. Marie bent down and helped Mama. 'As you know,' Mama said, 'Marie and I were nurses for the Russian soldiers in the Great War.' As they replaced the boot, light from one of the bonfires made a cross over the soldier's foot. The others gasped, crossed themselves instinctively with their big, bruised hands – and looked embarrassed.

As the wounded soldier stood up a tear dripped down his cheek; his lips looked like a baby's. A night of blackness had given way to a bright dawn. I was filled with light.

The love of the people will flow again. The hate sown by Trotsky and Lenin will go. Papa heard a rumour that Lenin has been in Petrograd since April.

I fill my mouth with Chateau Yquem, and taste the rich grapes. When I close my eyes I see meadows and fields and rivers. My sisters and I are dancing in white summer frocks as handsome young cavalry officers cheer us.

Soon we shall live in Somerset; Papa will be a farmer. King George will help us. I shall learn perfect English: 'China. Please. A crumpet? How delightful. What is the weather in your part of the country? Yes, next week Daddy is off to shoot grouses in Banffshire.' Czechoslovakian cavalry are massing on the border; Papa has heard that the White Army will charge through to save us.

In the bottom of my wine glass Rasputin's eyes are big as the globe. Rasputin first came to the Alexander Palace in 1905. He held Alexei's hand and Rasputin's eyes rolled: Alexei's bleeding stopped. Mama was overjoyed. She sat on

Alexei's bed and squeezed Rasputin's hand in the way she is squeezing Papa's now. Rasputin smiled at us and his look made silk walls you wanted to live inside. His eyes became spies in all our hearts.

A little wine has brought a tinge of joy to our cheeks. Tatiana does a jig around Alexei's bed, Papa finds a half-smoked cigar in his pocket and lights it. I think of the old days when he told us stories sitting round the fire, and I ask him to tell us one now, to keep away the wolves.

Alexei smiles as Tatiana teases him, but his brows are furrowed like an old man. He grips his silver cross with thin fingers. Nagorny, one of the two sailors who had looked after Alexei since he was very young, was shot last month when he stood in front of a Bolshevik solder who was trying to snatch Alexei's cross. Derevenko, Alexei's other sailor-helper, left soon after the revolution. He began shouting orders at Alexei, and taunting him.

How does hate enter the heart? What makes love stay? Holy Mother, bring back the love. Democracy was slowly coming to Russia: we had love not hatred.

A soldier comes in: 'Commandant Jacob Yurovsky to see you.'

Yurovsky enters. Tatiana stops dancing and sits on Alexei's bed. They hold hands and the silver cross flickers under their fingers.

'Orders,' Yurovsky says.' This way. Quick.'

Yurovsky's glasses rub on the bridge of his nose, making a red stain. They must be coming at last to exchange us.

The family follows Yurovsky downstairs, his uniform unpressed, his epaulette buttons tarnished. Our friends and helpers remain upstairs. Letts guards jostle us down the narrow stairs and into the cellar. I sit at the back and continue writing. A representative must be coming from England to negotiate our release – I knew King George would help – or perhaps the guards know the Czech troops are on their way. Thank you, Holy Mother!

'What!' Papa says, 'What!'

The Letts snort like pigs and raise their guns, point them. How they try to scare us! Every soldier has Rasputin's eyes and I hide my diary in the secret pocket of my skirt. I close my eyes: I am tobogganing at Tsarsko Selo; we are laughing in the cold air.

They fired the bullets through our flesh and left the shape of icons on the wall.

Christmas Games

When my father fell he cut open his head and I found him semiconscious in the cellar, his white shirt stained with blood. It was a stroke. After one week in intensive care at the Royal Surrey County Hospital in Guildford he went to a private nursing home in Windsor. It was early December 1966 and I was twelve-years-old. Father was twenty years older than my mother.

He had been at the nursing home for two days when Mother came up with one of her big ideas. She was putting on her morning face in front of the dressing-table mirror: 'Ronnie is over from Hollywood. He's filming and wants a decent place to live while he's here — it's urgent, shooting starts next week — and his company will pay a fortune, a little nest egg for us, darling, and it'll help Daddy. It's all so expensive.'

'You can't do that — I want to stay here — it's Christmas.'

She caressed her eyelashes with a black pencil.

'Daddy would hate it if we left. Look at me!' — she picked up a Chanel lipstick and I knocked it from her hand.

'How dare you.' She slapped my leg.

'You mustn't see Schmidt while Daddy is away.'

She put down her hairbrush and sat on the bed. 'Let's not get angry. Come here.' She hugged me and we lay down together.

A few days later at breakfast she told me a deal for our house had been arranged and we had somewhere else to go, 'A lovely place.' She took a parcel from a chair and put it on the table. I stared at my cornflakes. 'Open it then. I'm going shopping to Guildford. Mrs Dunnett will be here at 11. Bye.' She stood at the door. 'Don't worry about Mr Schmidt. I won't be seeing him again.'

In the corner of the brown packaging was 'Harrods'. I slid the knife around the edges, unpacked the Webley .177 air-pistol box, in which there was also a tin of pellets. I cleared away the breakfast things, then went outside and pinned a target to a box in front of the compost heap. I shot Schmidt six times as the sights weren't well adjusted and I wanted to make sure he was dead: three shots for me, three for my father. Mrs Dunnett did not like my mother but she loved my father; he always asked her advice about which tie to wear, and in return he gave her racing tips.

A week later the fat American lawyer with rubbery lips came down from London with the rental contract. You blushed as you stoked the fire. How well you played the role of supportive younger wife. He sipped a large whisky and sat in the best armchair, his gold-ringed fingers round my father's Stewart crystal tumbler.

Mrs Dunnett did most of the packing. Precious things went into storage. 'They want it furnished, darling; if they break the lot, hoorah. I'm sick of this museum.' You and I drove off in father's car, while Mrs Dunnett waved from the gate; you did not look back. More of our things were coming on later. We were going to a house in Ofsham for a few months.

It was a big ugly double-fronted gabled house near the station. There was a yellow front door, and bow windows with black frames. We had rented the top two floors. The granite outdoor stairs to our apartment were ingrained with whitish diamond flecks.

The Bauman sisters owned the house. Mother said that Miss Louise and Miss Marjorie were not married: 'They make dresses, haute couture; they once ran up something for the Queen!' We went to collect our keys and they stood together at the front door: Miss Louise had white streaks in her black hair; Miss Marjorie was younger and looked fitter; I thought she was in her fifties, but she was probably in her forties. They asked us to come for drinks that evening.

We hauled our cases up the stairs. I chose a bedroom on the top floor. Green paint was peeling off the ceiling; the sloped roof pressed down on me. But it was better than the room next door where the flock wallpaper hung loose and the plaster was cracked. From my small window I could make out the clock in the tower at Royal Holloway College. Mother had chosen a bedroom on the floor below. It was three days before Christmas. We spent the afternoon unpacking.

At six o'clock we knocked on the Baumans' front door. Miss Marjorie showed us in to the sitting room that smelt of mothballs. Miss Louise was in the high-backed armchair. When she smiled the doughy flesh on her face wobbled, and thick round glasses magnified her skin and eyes. A long pleated black skirt billowed over her body and legs. The thick gold plush velvet curtains were drawn. 'It's my eyes,' Miss Louise said, 'make yourselves comfortable.'

Miss Marjorie returned from the kitchen with a polished wooden tray and put it on top of the piano. Her black two-piece fitted tightly and her shiny stockings had seams up the back. She poured sherry and nimbly handed round the glasses, and a tumbler of orange juice for me. Her dark red lipstick glowed and her black-framed glasses had fins, studded with jewels 'What a lovely boy.' She put her face close: 'We want to make you happy, Simon, while you're here.' Her breath smelt of violets and her leg stretched against mine.

Miss Louise sat up, 'Don't embarrass the boy.' She pulled a brown tartan rug across her knees.

'You must tell me about the dress you made for the Queen,' Mother said but they talked about plumbing and bills and the odd habits of the bathroom door upstairs. They told Mother about Chilvers', the local butcher's, and Duncan, the greengrocer. As we got up to leave Miss Louise asked after my father.

I ran up the stairs and watched Mother reach the top flight — if I pushed her now she would tumble down and break a leg.

Ofsham was nowhere.

The next evening Miss Marjorie asked me down and made me hot chocolate in the cramped kitchen. 'Come on, let me show you the neighbourhood.' She took my arm and led me into her bow-windowed bedroom at the front of the house. She pulled back the net curtains: 'You can't see much in the street lamps but there used to be cows in that field; it was a very pretty.' Now it was a drab recreation ground and from the lights on Ofsham Station I could make out the empty swings which juddered in the wind. I sipped my drink and she sat on the bed. 'You need a favourite aunt while you are here. I'd love to make you a pair of trousers.' I peeled off the milk skin with the spoon and stirred hard. I drank it quickly and went upstairs.

In bed, the houses on either side pressed in on me. Far beneath my room sewing machines hummed and feet scurried like mice. I heard the phone ring.

The next morning at breakfast it was rainy dark and the windows rattled. When I thought of Great-Aunt Em or Aunt Rose or our house in Egford I only saw mist. Mother said she was sure it was nicotine stains on the dining room wall and not damp. We sat at separate ends of the table and she rubbed her hands together: 'Mr Schmidt and I have decided to be just friends. You don't want me to be lonely while I'm here?'

I said, 'You promised, promised,' and ran out. In my bedroom I read a Hardy Boys book. She never came up. My father sat at the end of my bed, a thin man smoking a cigarette.

When I went downstairs she was staring out of the sitting room window at the soaked back garden. 'Mummy,' I said, 'I understand, really.' She didn't turn but replied: 'I need a quiet Christmas, no relatives, nothing. I'm sorting

31

myself out.' Rain beat on the window. 'I need you, my lovely little man.' She kissed me.

A silver tree and decorations arrived from Caleys in Windsor. I helped set it up but each gold bauble I hung was a memory of the Christmas I was missing.

Upstairs I played with my Scalextric in the gloomy bedroom. I raced both cars at once, a controller in each hand. Schmidt's was a Porsche, mine a Brabham. I crashed him on the worst corner at Silverstone.

The next evening I answered the front-door and Karl Schmidt grinned at me: he was shiny from the glint of his blazer buttons to his spotty red silk tie. 'Hello, Simon, I am so sorry about your father.' I smelt his Aramis aftershave.

'How are your wife and two daughters, Mr Schmidt?'

'Simon; let Karl in.'

He pushed past me, kissed Mother and produced a bunch of flowers from behind his back, then a Selfridges carrier bag.

'Excuse me,' I said. I went downstairs because Miss Marjorie was making me a pair of green corduroy trousers and wanted me to try them on. I followed her into the large bedroom, the sewing machine in the corner. 'Sit on the bed for a minute,' she said. She reached into a cupboard, and slowly took out some pins. I could see down her cleavage. 'Stand up. I must measure you.' Up my inside leg the tape unwound. 'Very athletic.' She squeezed my thigh. 'You're a good cricketer, aren't you?' I got an erection. She measured my other leg. I thanked her and explained I must get back as I had to talk to my mother's friend.

Upstairs in the sitting room they were sipping reddish cocktails. 'How lucky,' Mother said, 'Karl is in England for Christmas and will be able to have lunch with us.' After I went to bed, I could hear them laughing. A whistle from an express train screamed in the distance. I thought about Father in the nursing home and eventually got to sleep.

The next morning the smell of Aramis was everywhere. I made my own breakfast. As I finished my Weetabix, Mother came in with a coffee, and we sat in silence.

That night, Christmas Eve, Miss Louise and Miss Marjorie asked us down for drinks. Louise wore the billowing black skirt but Miss Marjorie had on a black cocktail dress and puffed a Sobranie Black Russian through a gold cigarette holder. She brushed crumbs from my blazer — 'His socks need pulling up.' Her red fingernails pinched the back of my leg. 'Your trousers will be ready soon.'

'What service for little Lord Fauntleroy!' Mother said. 'An old friend is coming for lunch tomorrow. We're both delighted, aren't we?'

We stayed for over an hour.

On Christmas morning we visited Father. His bent fingers handed me a beautifully wrapped present; he gripped my hand, and blew his nose: 'You enjoy yourself, old chap. I'll be home soon.' As I left I knocked into the oxygen cylinder at the end of his bed. Mother and I returned to Ofsham in his car; his old tifter was on the rear-window ledge, a half-smoked cigar in the driver's ashtray. I stroked the red leather seat.

I followed her up the stairs. As she opened the front door the phone rang and she rushed up the corridor. 'No, Karl, no. You promised.' She stamped. 'You said you would never let me down again.' There was a pause. 'He's not coming, Simon — you've ruined it.'

At the sideboard in the dining room she poured a large gin and tonic, drank it in one and ran down the stairs. After half-an-hour she hadn't returned and I peered from every window. In my bedroom I knelt down and prayed to the Virgin Mary to bring her home safe and promised I would look after her. I made myself a fruit cocktail and put in a cherry on a stick. I stood by the Christmas tree and sang

'We wish you a merry Christmas and a happy New Year.' I finished my cocktail and kicked the presents under the tree.

Ten minutes later I answered the door and her arms were outstretched: 'I'm not going to spoil anything for you, darling.' In the evening Miss Marjorie came up with my trousers and insisted I try them on. I went into Mother's bedroom, got my old trousers off, and the door opened: 'That's a nice sight,' Miss Marjorie smiled. 'Mother heard and said, 'He's growing up fast!' They laughed. I scrambled into the corduroys. Miss Marjorie adjusted her glasses, 'Now do a fashion walk for us.'

I paraded past them as they lifted their Madeiras.

In January the new term began at my prep school.

Mother drove me there every morning but in the afternoons I came back on the train from Windsor and Eton Riverside station. Most mornings began in icy fog. As I left, Miss Marjorie often drew the curtains and blew a kiss. One day when I got home Mother was out and Miss Marjorie was in our kitchen. 'I'm going to cook your tea, Simon. Is there anything special you fancy?' She bent over the cooker; her white top was tight and I saw her nipples. like hard conkers through her thin bra; I tried to turn away but had to look; she stroked her leg; I walked out.

One afternoon in February Mother was crying again as she stared out of the window. 'It's over for ever. You may as well know, Simon. How unfair life has been to me.' She sprayed herself with Blue Grass, and kissed me.

When I went to bed the house creaked. Perhaps mother went out sometimes. In the night a hand touched mine. *Don't worry, Simon; don't feel lonely. A woman in a black nightdress sat on the edge of the bed. Her lipstick glistened as a hand reached under the covers.*

At school the next week we went on cross-country runs because the ground was too hard for rugby; I tried to remember my dream but I couldn't see it – I wanted to know, and didn't want to know, and wasn't sure anyway.

On Friday evening I returned from school and Mother had dressed up. She made bouillabaisse, chips, salad, and chocolate gateau. After dinner we played rummy in front of the fire. Mother was so beautiful. I won and then we watched Steptoe and Son. 'We must stick together, my darling boy.'

In the night a woman was at my bedroom door, then touched my knee, pulled down the covers and said, 'I am so lonely, so afraid', got into bed, held me against her flimsy black nightdress.

The next morning Mother cooked me bacon and tomatoes.

In the first week of February snow fell for two days and I couldn't get to school. Mother loved 'weather'. We dressed up and trudged through the snow to Aunt Rose's house in Virginia Water. Our footprints made connections to the roads, paths and fields of my real world. Ronnie finished filming and returned to Hollywood.

We returned to Egford: Miss Marjorie and Mother embraced before we got into our car, as if they were friends. 'And if you need alterations to those lovely trousers, drop in.' She kissed my ear, and her tongue licked. My father came out of the nursing home in March. A week later I was sitting on a stool in the kitchen, and eating a slice of Mother's jam sponge cake.

'Giles is coming round this afternoon for cricket practice.'

'Lovely, darling. You have such nice friends.'

I watched her bend over the washing machine and put in towels and sheets. Tucked between the pillowcases I could see a black nightdress. I got up and gave her a push. She fell on the polished floor, her diamond ring scraping the parquet, her mouth gaping. I ran out.

A few weeks later they sent me to see a psychiatrist and he suggested I should go to boarding school.

Terry

When it rains in Salford I can taste salt in the raindrops, you know, when you put your head up. I love sitting by the window in the front room in the dark.

It's started to drizzle and the days are drawing in. I think it's the chemical factory, that's where I worked since school, two A levels. Once I moved out of home for a month but something pulled me back. I was always Mother's little Terry, but sitting here I feel myself. Twenty-five-years a technician at the chemical factory isn't everyone's idea of an exciting life, but it suited me, all in all. I'm set in my ways, I know that.

And since Mother died, two years this September, I've slowed up. I've done some tidying on the house, a Victorian terrace, but otherwise I've been rather quiet.

'Just do that for me will you, Terry love?' Ooh, there was no end to it.

I don't go out much, but I'm free inside now, that's the difference. I get on very well with the neighbours — Bola, she's Nigerian. They moved in last year. I had a dinner round there recently, very interesting. And she wears the most lovely clothes, multicoloured material that wraps round and round. They brought some colour to the street.

Time I thought of something for tea. On a Friday I often have a takeaway; there's a lovely Indian on the corner of Maygrove Street, but I'm feeling rather withered, you know. I might just take a mozzarella and ham pizza from the freezer and watch a video. Why not? I'm my own master now.

I love Marilyn Monroe. I'll watch *Some Like it Hot* tonight; that's one of her best, 1959. And all those cheeky chaps dressing up as women. Marlon and Clint, the budgies, are making such a racket behind me, but I'm very fond of them. They keep fit and we make each other laugh.

I'm going to Knutsford on Sunday, lunch with Veronica, my big sister. It's good to get out. She was a dental nurse, married the dentist, Derek Palmer. His family are from Lytham, near the golf course. She must have given him laughing gas before he agreed. No children.

It's a bloody ugly street, there's no denying that.

'Come fair bombs and fall on Salford.'

There were never much beauty in our family. Father worked in the power station, stoked boilers or summat like. He looked like a boiler too. Had this very loud voice and shouted 'Hey up' down the street to his mates. I don't think he'd ever heard of art or film stars. He followed rugby league. Every time he came back from a match, it was 'Do you good, bit of rugby. You're too soft, lad.'

I was always a thin boy, willowy, and I liked to wear my dark hair a bit long. I thought I looked nice when I smiled into the mirror after a bath, and held the little towel tight around my waist. I've hazel eyes and I'd pucker my lips like a film star.

If you sprinkle a little parsley on a pizza, it's very nice. I'll have a few glasses of Soave. Why not? I'm not short of a few bob.

I do watercolours in my spare time. I might take it further one day. Dad smoked forty a day, drank stout. Over twenty-years-ago the old boiler just blew up, heart attack, Saturday afternoon, after his team, Wigan, had lost to St. Helens. It was a blessing, all in all.

Greta Garbo is my favourite, that feeling for the camera, those wonderful dresses, that face. *Camille*, *Anna Karenina*. I know every scene by heart. 'You shouldn't watch them so much,' Mother used to say, 'Get out more.' But if I did she was the first to moan.

Just before Mother died I had trouble at work. Some of the lads started to taunt me. It seemed to be raining all the time and Mother had just been diagnosed. I'd got too friendly with Jimmy, a young boy in accounts. Made a fool of myself. I'd never encouraged that side of me before.

'Quiet down, Marlon!'

I had this recurring idea that when God made the earth he gave Salford to the devil to play with; it was that ugly. I used to cry myself to sleep at night in the back room and imagine the clogs of the dead shuffling to work. And Mother used to stare at me.

Oh goodness! I thought I saw her coming down the street then. Sometimes I'm convinced it's her, or me Dad – and then I'm so pleased it can't be. Wicked, I know but she wouldn't understand.

The doctor gave me anti-depressants, but I didn't want to talk. On the way out, he said: 'There's nothing wrong, you know, your erotic feelings, nothing wrong at all.'

'How dare you!'

But the doctor's words kept repeating in my mind. What a nerve! When I got home I put on *Anna Karenina* to calm me down. I have a very high-quality DVD. Garbo was wearing a long silky dress and I could feel its softness on my legs and thighs. I saw Dad in the mirror: 'You're too quiet, lad.' He was a bully and everything about him was ugly, ugly, ugly.

It's almost dark now, but I feel so bright inside these days.

Anyway, after coming back from the doctor's, I couldn't settle to the film. I went into the spare-room wardrobe where Veronica, my sister, had left a lot of her things. My heart was racing. I tried a dress, then a skirt and a slip. I felt so nice, so right, and I burst into a flood of tears.

I just sat there in front of the mirror, making up with a bit of old eyeliner and lipstick I'd found in the bottom of the wardrobe. Then I went downstairs and watched the rest of *Anna Karenina* again.

I'll pour myself a glass of that Soave and sit here for another ten minutes before I draw the curtains. I'm going to paint the windows before the winter. I do it all myself.

After my first dressing up, I bought a wig and other bits and pieces.

At the end of our street there's a big billboard with Marilyn Monroe advertising cigarettes, and drinking a glass of champagne in the moonlight.

Oh, that's lovely wine. I'm wearing my black cocktail dress tonight, blonde wig, nicely made-up. I could almost be there, in that advertisement, drinking champagne. I'd call myself Jasmine.

When I'm like this, I'm me, only me: I've got no family, no Mother looking over me like I'm a bad smell. I'm just Jasmine and I don't have any past at all.

I'm happy sitting here. It's not a bad life, all in all, looking up at Marilyn. It's started to drizzle. Marilyn's lower lip is tilted upwards. I wonder if she can taste salt in the raindrops too?

Swimming with Diana Dors

I watched from behind a rhododendron bush. She pointed the hose at the pool and spray rose to make a fuzzy rainbow beneath the high trees. The nozzle slipped and wet her green slacks. She screamed and kicked off her yellow sandals. I sank back into the shrubbery and knocked over my bike.

'Who's there?'

The hose hissed.

'Who is it?'

She walked down the side of the pool.

'Sorry, it's me. I'm a friend of Ti Wells.' I crawled through and stood up. 'I was hiding my bike. He's not in.'

'You're Stephen, aren't you? Last week I gave your tennis ball back.'

'Yes. I'm awfully sorry.'

Diana Dors laughed through red lips and her teeth sparkled. 'Turn off the tap, will you?' She nodded in the direction of a wooden shed. I ran over.

'Thanks.' She dropped the hose into the pool but her wavy ash-blonde hair stayed in place. 'Sit down and have a drink. I'll get changed. Look through that lot if you want, cuttings of me; my agent told me to get organised.'

I perched on the lime-green lounger. Her bottom swayed and the line of her knickers showed through. Pine trees grew in a square around the ranch-style house and bubbly clouds passed over the blue sky as if they were on a television screen.

I poured orange juice from the stripy glass jug and undid the buttons of my Aertex shirt. My father would be cross if he knew I was here. Last night he said the country was going to the dogs, 'But what can you expect when you put that Catholic Itie Profumo in the cabinet?' I should be doing homework — I would never get into my father's Oxford college if I carried on like this — and how would he punish me this time? Mother said I should be allowed more fun but he told her off and she went upstairs to cry again.

As I closed my eyes, sun soaked into me; I flicked through the snippets: 'Diana Dors, a Rank starlet', 'Diana Dors buys a Rolls', 'Diana to storm Hollywood', on and on, always with pictures of her, some in bikinis. I stroked her lying on a red velvet sofa.

'That's a good one,' she said, 'he got me just right.'

She had changed into a swimming costume.

'My father said you were very good in *The Hitchcock Hour* last week.'

She leaned over me. 'But you prefer me like that?' She directed my finger on to the glossy page.

'My father said you could be a very good actress, I mean...'

'I'm a professional, Stephen. I trained at LAMDA. What do you think I am?' She poured juice into her glass and then caressed the silver pattern along the top-half of her costume. 'I was hoping for a dip. Do you live in Virginia Water?'

'No, in Thorpe.' Juice dribbled down my front.

'I'm only renting; a man or the taxman will probably drive me on again.'

She clicked a gold lighter and lit a Winston. I've given up smoking, don't tell.'

'Of course not.'

My father said he could never live on the Wentworth Estate or 'Hollywood-by-the-lake'. He thought it a good joke and Mother and I laughed too. But I had known Ti since I was five when we were at Virginia Water Junior School. Next door to Diana, Ti's parents had a huge mock-Georgian house.

She put her lips carefully round the rim of the cup, and left no lipstick marks.

'You could swim too.'

'I didn't bring trunks.'

Her pink tongue licked her top teeth like a lizard. She danced off. I should tell my father that I don't bloody care about homework. What could he do? A few minutes later she came back dangling a pair of trunks and the ends of the tie-up cord did a somersault and looped together.

'You're very handsome when you smile. Stand up.' She held the bright red trunks against me. 'See if they fit. I bought them in Hollywood because they reminded me of Rock Hudson — he's so butch.' She looked into my eyes and her long black eyelashes clicked up and down.

I stepped back. 'All right.'

She rested her hand on my shoulder as she led me through the French windows. 'Use the spare bedroom down the long corridor, first on left. Call me Diana.' She picked up a magazine from the coffee table and went out.

The room was white with a double bed covered in a white silk sheet and matching pillows. I watched myself undress in the long gold-framed mirror. Two weeks ago, at Ti's house, I was scrabbling in the bushes for our tennis ball; I peered into Diana's house and she was changing in the sitting room, unbuckling her bra strap, when Ti called 'Found it!' — and I ran back to the tennis court.... I pulled the trunks slowly up my body.

When I went out Diana was sitting on the lounger and she whistled, 'Fhewfhew'. I knotted my hands across my front.

'Come on!' she said. We jumped in. 'Keep to the left, the other side hasn't been cleaned.'

Her breast-stroke was very good, and she didn't care when her hair was wet. We swam for ages.

'Time to get out.' She picked up a light-blue towel from the side and rubbed me dry. She handed it to me: 'Can you do my back?'

I patted her and rubbed slowly when I reached the top of her shoulders.

We flopped on the loungers, a wicker table between us, and I turned quickly onto my stomach.

She leaned on her elbow: 'The Wellses have gone to Harrods for English tea and Marmite before they head across the pond — they have a summer place in the Hamptons.'

'I know. A few years ago Ti had suggested I might go with them.'

'But you haven't?'

'No.'

He's a nice boy and his father is divine, but that mother — what a bitch.'

'Crikey, not really.' I swiped at some gnats.

'Don't you ever think bad things?' She giggled.

'Not much.' I walked over to the dark corner of the garden where weeds were thick between the bedding plants. When I met Ti's father he would pump my hand, his crew-cut bristling with shine, and talk fast through his big smile. His eyes always swivelled beyond me, as if I wasn't quite enough. He made you feel good though, like drinking strong coffee.

'Mrs Wells scares me.'

'Turn round. Tell me, not the garden.'

'Since I was five when you eat there she gives you huge portions and a tall glass of milk and if you don't finish every morsel you've failed.' I paused. 'And she judges me and I always fail — and she's as cold as their ginormous American fridge — no, worse — she's an Ice Queen!'

Diana clapped. 'Bet you feel better.'

She ran in and put on a record and two big speakers blasted out the sound. 'It's Billy Fury's "Half Way to Paradise".' It's a few years old but I love it. Can you do The Twist?'

'Gosh, no, not properly.'

43

She swished to the music. 'You need more fun. What does your father do?'

'He's a circuit judge.'

'A few judges have circuited me in my time. I never do well in law courts.'

I lay down and smiled at her. Last holidays he took me to see him in court and we sat in the back of the Daimler as the chauffeur drove us to Winchester. Father took out court papers from his black briefcase and stared at me over half-rimmed glasses: 'Why don't you get on with your Latin homework, Stephen?' His lips smiled as if stretching for exercise and then sprung back into a grimace. The prisoner in the dock, with his greasy dark quiff, said something about his alibi, a blousy girl, 'my bit on the side'. My father asked for clarification and gave him that smile. The man got four years for burglary.

'Come on, I'll teach you,' she said, 'listen to this, "The Twist". It's the B side of a Hank Ballard single. This is the Sixties!'

She flipped her hair as she danced on the patio like she was in a nightclub. She held out her hands and I tried to follow how her body moved but my legs were wood.

'You're not watching me enough.' She pulled me to her, and shook my hips from side to side. 'Now you're moving!'

My fingers rested on her shoulders as our bodies gyrated. 'No, I can't do it properly.' I pulled away and blushed.

She lifted the stylus from the record and touched her lips: 'I think you can do it very well. Don't worry. Okay, I'll show you how to make a good drink.'

Inside the long room, furniture and chairs were bright and modern and low to the ground. The polished wooden floor reflected our shadows. She tossed me a cocktail shaker which I just caught, and we stood by the gold trolley with two shelves loaded with bottles of every shape, colour and size. Gadgets shone like a surgeon's tools.

'This is my favourite just now,' she said, 'A New York Cocktail.'

She held the *Savoy Cocktail Book* in front of me. Above the garden puff clouds vibrated as if the day itself was swimming. Ice cubes, a sugar lump, De Kuyper Grenadine, Canadian Club whiskey, mixed in the shaker. Diana squeezed lime and cut orange peel.

'Hold it up,' she said.

I shook it above my head. She copied my actions and we laughed.

'That's enough.' She came closer, took it from my hands, and licked off beads of ice bubbles. Diana poured the colourful liquid into her cocktail glass, and filled mine half full. 'It doesn't taste like Scotch at all.'

We sat outside and the sun had come back.

'Are you afraid of fun?'

'No.'

But I was. I loved her life, drinks and dancing, swims and parties.

'Do you have girlfriends?'

'Not really.'

'When I lived in Watford, the American GIs whistled. I was thirteen and had a good figure. They called me Veronica Lake. They took me to their dances. I looked much older.'

The New York Cocktail made my head float. She puffed up the turquoise cushion behind my head.

'Are you going on holiday this summer?' she asked.

'Don't know.' I gulped down my drink and jumped into the pool. Last Wednesday I went in to the study to take my father his favourite Hine brandy in the Waterford crystal balloon glass I had bought for his birthday. I quietly made my case that we all needed a break. He said, 'You should be thinking of more important things, don't you agree?' I closed the door quietly. He went on reading through one of his judgements.

45

I leaned my elbows on the pool side: 'My father doesn't let mother and me go any more – Uncle David, one of my father's friends, took us two years running on his boat around Cornwall. It was heaven.'

'Your poor mother.'

'He was my father's friend. Mother cries a lot.'

When I got out Diana hugged me to her springy flesh. 'I need to sort your father out!' She bounced away.

'Please don't.'

'Do you like me?'

'I hardly know you.'

'You like watching me.'

'I didn't mean to.'

'No harm in looking.'

I spread the towel on the lounger and lay on my stomach. Last October Uncle David had gone to Argentina to help an old friend who had cattle and a corned-beef factory. Now David was very ill in a Buenos Aires hospital and Mother had heard nothing for a month.

'I'll tell you something. My real name is Fluck and I never even thought my father was my father. They made me change my name – imagine 'Fluck' up in lights outside a theatre and the bulb blows in the L – doesn't bear thinking about.'

'I see what you mean!'

'Why don't you and your mother go and live without Oliver Cromwell? You'd both be happy.' She went inside and beckoned me with her finger from behind the window. 'Come on, and I'll show you another secret.'

Down the long corridor was a large room off to the right with a curtain along the side. She went in: 'Pull it back.'

I tugged – the wall was a mirror. You saw through to the other side. 'Watch this.' She jumped up and down on the bed, came out and pinched my cheek. 'My friends really like it. You mustn't tell anyone.'

'Never.'

'Looking is nice. Do you want a go and I'll watch you?'

It was a springy bed. 'Yippee!' I said and leapt like a trampoline star. 'It's great, great.' I bounced down flat on my back and got off, raised my arms and bowed to her in the corridor. 'Shall we jump on it together, Diana?'

'You're a naughty boy.' She stroked my back. The front-door bell chimed. 'Who the hell's that?'

'If it's the taxman, I'll help you out!'

'That's better, you're relaxing; go and sit in the lounge, won't be a minute.'

She went off down the other side of the L-shaped corridor which formed part of the square round the house.

'Larry! What are you doing?'

'Just been to Wembley Studios for a part in *No 'Iding Place*; I'm the getaway driver, then I'm off to Southampon, two days filming.'

'Come in.'

He stood at the door. 'This your new 'usband?'

He strode towards me; he was tall and strong with black hair, sideboards, very blue eyes and a red Hawaiian shirt. I got up.

' 'Ello son,' he shook my hand, 'You a neighbour?'

'Not exactly.'

'You acting with her?'

Diana tapped his arm. 'Don't quiz him, Larry. He's a new friend, Stephen; I threw back his tennis ball last week.'

'Very nice.'

His black suede pointed shoes turned neatly on the floor and he sat down.

'I'll fix you a drink. Usual?' She gently pulled his hair, then moved over to the drinks' trolley.

'Please.'

'Tell me about yourself, son.' He glanced down the corridor. 'What you been showing him?' He laughed.

'Nothing at all,' I said.

She handed him a tumbler of whisky on the rocks, and massaged his neck. 'You must be tired,' she said.

We all went outside and sat down.

Her teeth sparkled when she smiled at Larry. I noticed a large leaf in the pool, which reminded me of Uncle David's boat as it chopped through the gushing waves into Penzance harbour; he had said to me, 'You only have one life, Stephen. Follow your dream.'

'Have one more swim if you want.' Diana looked at her watch.

'Thank you.'

She turned away.

I dived in and she called, 'Watch out that side, the pump's not working.' I race-crawled until slime covered my forearm. I grabbed the edge. Mosquitoes hovered above the green greasy film.

'It's nothing to worry about as the man's coming tomorrow.'

'I've come early! ' Larry said.

Between the paving stones, cigarette ends — a pink one, a yellow one, a black one — were trodden down. Lipstick stains on the gold filters had stained brown in the damp. I jumped out of the pool and she said if I wanted to serve drinks when they next had a party I could make some pocket money. The dark fir trees took away all views except for the television-screen square of sky above this cowboy homestead, lost in the wrong country.

I got out and dried myself, ran in to the house, changed quickly, and joined them by the pool. 'Thank you very much, Diana, but I've got to go now.'

She kissed me on both cheeks.

'I wouldn't mind a swim,' Larry said.

'I'll get you some trunks in a minute; I think I can find a pair that fits.'

'He must come again, mustn't he?' Larry pointed at me.

Gravel crunched on the road. I peered through the rhododendrons. The Wellses' cream Jaguar Mark X was sailing along, the white trim round the tyres making the car look presidential. Mrs Wells got out of the back seat and stepped towards the front door with keys in her hand. Mr Wells opened the boot and Ti stood with him. A noise in the trees made them look up and Ti now had the stare of his father, seeking into the distance for something new to conquer.

I waved to Diana. She blew me a kiss and dropped a cigarette end. Ti and his father took parcels into the house. I cycled off as I needed to do homework.

Ben

Early, but I'm awake. Daffodils on the windowsill are wilting, but I won't replace them until I have fresh ones. Robin is snoring, move your legs! No children calling yet, ten more minutes, not growing younger; in spring the world is young but I'm not. Toby, Amy, and Ben, the eldest – he's such hard work, but now he's at special school we get more help – and God forgive me for not loving him more. Toby and Amy I love to death. I do my best. Lord Darnley is waiting for the oak dining table that Robin is making; such a special commission; why won't he get on?; he's so bloody slow, and this old creaky house goes on creaking – I'll sort it out he said, and make it lovely, all the space....

I'm not young, but men look, and the postman undressed me with his gull's eyes, on the doorstep. I smiled a bit; I know he was fucking me, on the doorstep, as he got me to sign for the Registered Letter, and I fucked him back; he knew. Lucky girlfriend! I've seen her, all legs and blonde hair, and it's no wonder she's always smiling. Is that Amy coughing, my little poppet? Too early, not yet darling.

I'm not depressed this year; I imagine bulbs popping up the hill on either side of the high valley; I see so far from here, flowers on the hillside, a world of colour – last year, so low, black shadows creeping up the hill like tar, and the sun was black. Why?

Robin said see a therapist, but someone gave me daffodils and my spirit turned. I was well again; I thanked God. When I did bell-ringing I was the sound of all things and all joy for weeks, never again so low. Please God. Robin, now! All right. You're so hard, won't last long in the morning. Yes, I'm ready, yes, yes, yes – those thrusts too soon spent – there, there; I wish he'd gone on.

Amy's clothes over the bathroom, but it's home, it's mine, Amy get your clothes on, no you can't have a bath now, Ben, stop dreaming, clean your teeth, get your homework, Ben, get dressed! I'm not being impatient Robin, then *you* bloody well dress him. Ben pull your trousers up, now hold hands tightly on the way to school. No, Ben, the special bus is coming for you. Yes, thank you Robin, more tea please, and work hard on that table today. We need the money.

The sky is blue against the dark valley sides. In the spring I am the yolk of an egg, in our big mill house, and the valley is the egg's white, spreading up the sides; lilies of the valley, part of us, of me, life, the cold new sun. Hoover, clean, feed the chickens, pick parsley for the sauce tonight. Robin is cooking fish, and he's good like that; I hope he gets on today; at university I loved the spring, the students in my year, together, sitting around, talking. There was never anything you couldn't do. Now I live in a green valley, must get out more.

Lovely coffee, reading in the afternoon, with the window open, Robin working; I wonder how Amy's art lesson went? She loves art, and Toby knows so much about nature, such bright children. Ben is our cross; I'm sorry God, must bear it better. Poor boy. I'm reading Virginia Woolf again, *To the Lighthouse*, it's so fine; my body is touching my dress, going hot, my nipples hard, perhaps tonight, Robin, slowly, long and slow. Sometimes you get it right.

Toby and Amy are home, playing together; I love them together; a different family when Ben isn't here. How horrible. What a thing to say. Poor Ben. But Toby and Amy playing together, lovely; yes fish fingers, yes chips, yes beans — what a lovely painting, Amy, and you wrote a story about a tree? Toby and Ben don't spit out your food, don't grab, wretched boy — I'm not being unfair Robin.

Robin and I sit with drinks, in the little sitting room which we try to keep clear, the children in bed, as the brook bubbles through the weir; we listen, not hearing, pebbles, as the brook funnels its way through and pools in the little lake above. And we are pebbles listening. Ghosts of the village listen as the brook bubbles forever, and we shall listen till we hear no more. No, I'll have wine with my supper, Robin. No more now, thank you.

I'll go for a short walk if you don't mind, a short walk before dark, and already the night is flapping down the valley like a giant gull's wing. I walk up the darkening wooded slope of West Hill, towards the last light, so much life in me; slowly up, as my heart pounds with the steps, with the life in me, with my dress that touches all the curves of me. He's there!

'Take me, take me now,' I say.

Deep shaft of sun, as the light dies, inside me, slow, the rhythm of the sun's shaft, his gull's eyes and big, fresh face, looking into me, fucking me more and more, the sun in me, forever, as he pounds my thighs to earth, leaves and mulch, his eyes fucking me, until I die as the sun dies, no shadows on us, in the early dark, clear.

My legs tremble as I climb down the hill, past the church my spirit trembles, and God should understand. I rattle the catch. Won't be a moment, Robin, and tomorrow I will be kind to Ben. I place fresh daffodils in the vase on the bedroom window.

Storm at Galesburg

Steel-sharp Chicago wind scattered Richard's thoughts to all quarters and cold air tore through his dark-blue Aquascutum overcoat as he followed Eugene to the Oldsmobile station wagon. Richard felt the lines of his face and rubbed his hand across his cheeks. The car was parked a few blocks away from the Union League Club, Chicago, where Richard had been staying during the conference. The tall quietly-grand buildings reassured him about something he could not define.

'It's a very comfortable car,' Eugene said and Richard heard the sentence in staccato bursts, as if each word had to struggle through the maelstrom.

The passenger seat was strewn with papers and cigarette packets; dogs' hairs stuck to the material. With a flash of hands Eugene tidied up and grabbed a few parcels from the floor. 'Samples. Cattle feed is a scientific business — "Try Before You Buy!" is my catchphrase — and it works most of the time. Guess I should retire soon.' His chunky face puckered up. 'Get in, get in.'

Richard smiled thinly, held his suitcase tight, and wished he had taken the plane.

'I'll put that in the trunk.'

'Thank you.'

Richard sat in the passenger seat and medicinal aromas mixed with stale sweat; he put his hand over his nose and opened the window. Why didn't I bloody well fly! he thought. Lisa, the secretary to the academic conference, had arranged for Eugene, her brother, to give Richard a lift. 'How lucky you're going to the same place,' she had said through her super-bright smile, and told him, with that unsullied innocence he admired in Americans, about her two children, a boy and a girl, who were both at college and doing so well.

'All done.' Eugene sat in the driver's seat.

His head moved quickly, like a boxer determined to get across his punches, and his white-grey hair was in crew-cut style. I'm probably envious, Richard chastened himself, and saw Eugene in a world of families and American football games, hot dogs and manicured lawns.

'My cell phone's not working,' Eugene said, 'got one?'

'It broke down too. My spare is in England.'

'We'll just keep our fingers crossed.'

They set off. Razorblade wind cut through the iron-grey sky and the car veered slightly. Richard's spirits rallied when he thought of yesterday's accolades after his talk. And a preppy, darkly attractive young man, a PhD student at Princeton, had said to him: 'Professor Woodward, I so enjoyed your lecture yesterday.' Richard recalled his smile, and those green eyes that had blinked knowingly. He wished he had pursued the brief encounter.

No, life was good, if a little lonely, but could he bear it any other way? The car's heater thawed him out. He folded his overcoat and placed it carefully on the back seat.

'I'm going to Galesburg on business,' Eugene said from out of the car's darkness, 'glad to be of help.'

'I'm very grateful.'

Richard felt guilty about his reservations and smiled too eagerly. This encouraged Eugene to share his views about American kids having it too easy and how it wasn't like that for him when he was a boy in Des Plaines. As an adult, Eugene had lived all over, Cincinnati, Denver, Chicago, and now had almost retired 'to a little place in Thedford, Nebraska, near where my wife's family came from, Norwegians originally, cattle farmers – you got to keep moving, you know, stay young!'

'I dare say.'

Richard locked his hands together. How big America felt, how rootless, while his own life was a sort of English B road existence, but that's what he liked, the quiet, private connoisseurship of studying ancient things. Richard made an effort to be sociable, talked about history and identity, 'What it was to be English' and 'How history has been largely forgotten'. Eugene embraced the idea with American enthusiasm: 'You never said a truer word. Kids don't understand. You say "Second World War" to them – I said to my son, "It's you, it's your history. Remember" – he stared at me like I was goofy.'

The rhythm of the roads soothed them and they sank into private reflections.

'Crackers in the glove box if you're hungry,' Eugene said after a while.

The confident architecture gave way to areas where paint was flaking off the dingy houses. They reached the suburbs: every house with a large front garden, every lawn green and trimmed.

'Live in London, Richard?'

'Flat near the British Museum,' he said, but his visual recollection of his home was weak, as if he was telling a scene from a novel he didn't much like. He pinched his hand, touched his top pocket, but the handkerchief Tom had given him was gone.

'You okay?' Eugene asked.

'Forgot something, not important.' His heart raced and America felt vast and unknown, as if the car was adrift on a sheet of ice at the North Pole.

Eugene whistled, tapped the steering-wheel, fiddled with the radio, 'It's really crackly, as the weather's bad, but we'll get through.'

Richard envied that American spirit, the confidence of moving forward, of getting there, but he wanted some peace now, time to think. Eugene burbled on, about his children, both grown up: Sandie who lived in Normal,

Illinois and was a teacher; she married an electrician who's got his own business. Christ, Richard thought, I could have written the script myself; he's going to tell me about his homemade apple pie any minute. Richard yawned. Eugene's son, Lee, was in Chicago, ran a bar, bit of a bum. 'But Jodie, that was my wife... she died last year, cancer... together thirty-seven years.' He blew his nose.

'I'm sorry.'

Richard looked distractedly out of the passenger window and his reflection dissolved into a trickle of rust over snow. He sucked hard on a mint, and tried to bring back an image of himself in the glass.

Eugene had quarrelled with both his children, but Sandie was a nice girl. 'I want to apologise to Sandie; life's too short.'

The long freeway opened up. Snow fell hard and giant bright trucks seared like silver ghosts across America. Where did they come from, these lithe, roaring spectres? Where were they were going? Richard patted his racing heart.

'You married?' Eugene asked.

'Confirmed bachelor. I was an only child, and grew to prefer my own company.'

'Jesus! Why can't you Brits spit it out?'

'I don't know what you mean.'

'If you're fucking gay, say so — who cares?'

'I beg your pardon.'

'You heard.'

'I've no idea why you make that assumption. It's of no interest to anyone, nor is it true.'

'My sister told me. Everyone in the organisation knows. No one minds. Only you.'

'I should have gone by plane.'

'You think I don't know you're treating me like a low life.' Eugene jerked his head at Richard. 'I'm direct, that's all.'

The car snaked into another lane.

'Watch out!' Richard screamed.

'Screw you.'

From under the seat Eugene drew out a revolver, and held it high. With the other hand he straightened the car.

'Stop!' Richard squealed.

'I'm direct, that's all.' Eugene laughed and replaced the gun beneath the seat.

They drove in silence until Eugene crooned a Johnny Cash song, 'On the Evening Train'; then he told Richard about his poor Polish parents, his father, who was a baker with three shops, and Eugene's mom ran one of them, as if those facts were an extension of the song's elegy.

Richard pretended not to listen. 'I suppose you think your rude violence has scared me? Perhaps that's how America always wins her wars.'

'I meant no harm. Life's not been easy just now. I'm not always truthful with myself — if you'd just said, "Sure, I'm gay".'

'A moment ago you were trying to kill me.'

'Don't exaggerate. Pass me that Hershey's bar.'

They stopped at a diner for lunch. Snow was thick in the parking area.

Half an hour later Eugene returned excitedly from the gents, 'We'd better push on. A trucker told me the electricity is down in Galesburg; the storm just blew it all out.'

Eugene put the heater up to high. The windscreen was almost blanked-out white as if they were alone and estranged in an igloo. All the cars' headlights were on, like a thousand double spears of light probing the dark. Eugene hummed and then talked about his dead wife, Jodie, and her pink bath cap, which he found behind the shower-room door, 'Been there over a year, never noticed it until that moment.'

'It's not that I'm gay, you see. I simply don't have relations, period, as you would put it.'

'If that's how you want it.'

'I live quietly. I'm a natural solitary. Strange, I know.' And Tom probably won't be in touch again, he thought.

'I need people. I feel old and lonely these days.'

'May I have a cracker?'

Richard nibbled loudly: he had no wish to listen to a stranger's confessions. He tightened the knot of his tie.

All the trucks and cars slowed. A blast of snow covered the windscreen, which intensified the hushed rumble from the world outside. A few miles on and the police were busily directing the traffic. Eugene's eyes scanned a bigger darkness, beyond the shopping malls, McDonalds, TVs and American football. 'Business isn't what it was. I really must retire early, settle in Nebraska.'

Nebraska, Richard whispered, Nebraska, Nebraska, Nebraska.

'Look, no more road lights. That trucker was right — the power has gone.'

Vehicles moved forward like a long trail of settlers seeking somewhere new to start again. Ten minutes later the traffic stopped. Eugene felt beneath his seat because this was America and the lights were out.

Richard's clammy fingers instinctively checked his top pocket, but there was no handkerchief.

'We'll be there soon,' Eugene said. 'Someone picking you up?'

'I have to phone from the call-box on the corner of Broad Street. The dean will send someone for me.'

At the outskirts of Galesburg, the radio told them that bad weather was coming down all the way from Canada. They reached the middle of town. Eugene stopped the car but kept the engine running.

His warm eyes looked into Richard's: 'Some beautiful old trains in Galesburg, used to connect America, right down to Santa Fe.' Eugene held out his thick hand. 'Maybe the lights will come back soon. We had a disagreement. I'm sorry. Let's move on.'

'I'll be fine, thank you. Very interesting drive.'

As Richard stood on the pavement he tugged his overcoat collar tight against the blizzard. The passenger door shut with a thud; Eugene set off and his tail-lights bobbed into the distance like illuminated buoys among drifts of swirling snow.

Rays of light from the candlelit bars showed the name 'Broad Street'. He could just make out a line of wood-panelled shops. At the end of the road an organ was booming from a large church. Wind chopped at him from all sides and his fingers dug into his empty top pocket.

From the call-box he dialled quickly as snow fell.

The Gardener

Mr Carver came up Willetts Lane to our cottage in November 1961. It was just me and Izzie, my younger sister, since Mum was taken in 1951, a week before the Festival of Britain. His good sports jacket hung off his bones. 'I've heard, Mr Rhodes, you may be looking for a little extra gardening work.'

'You heard right, sir.'

We shook hands and came to an understanding. I liked him straight off, a quiet gentleman, rather withered considering his young wife and boy. I couldn't imagine he could cope with her; there was a lot of gossip in the village. Izzie stood on the porch, drizzle trickling from her hair and down her nose. She looked more like Mum than ever, her body all good health.

I cycled down to the Carvers the next Sunday morning. It was an old Victorian place, double-gabled, with an acre and a half at the back. They had a regular gardener, Bill Cranham, but he'd slipped a disc. I took a couple of geraniums from my greenhouse, and a few cuttings from a Fuchsia Mantilla, one of my favourite varieties.

'Oh, thank you, Will; you are too kind,' Mrs C said all la-di-da. She looked a lady, and had good legs. She'd been on the stage, and Mr Hitchcock had used her in one of his films. She was too friendly for a first meeting. Last June I saw Colonel Prideaux's Jaguar come out of her drive, a sultry day, just after my dinner time. He was known to have an eye for the ladies, and them for him. I knew the governor was away on business. Maybe nothing in it.

The garden was in a right old state! It had been landscaped in the Twenties, I remember my dad talking, but it hadn't come to much. Mr Carver walked me round, and Simon, the boy, was introduced: 'How do you do, Mr

Rhodes,' he said, and shook my hand. He was only seven, a fine little fellow.

Those first months were just clearing out. Some lads from the village gave a hand. By February of '62 we'd made progress. Izzie cooked lovely casseroles that winter, hares, pheasant, scrag-end of neck, rabbit, vegetables, plenty of root crops. Some said she was a bit simple. But she was a good girl, lovely smile. We were as snug as bugs. I never looked seriously for a wife, and now I'm middle-aged, I don't know that I feel like one; Mum used to say they were all trollops round here.

In March we could think of planting out for the spring. Mr Carver came round the garden. 'That's a good idea, Will, to make more variety in that border.' Simon darted in and out of the shrubbery, playing cowboys. I wrote down a few plants: lupins, stocks, sweet peas, osteospermum. Mr Carver and me were much of a mind. 'Must consult my wife, of course.' He stroked his white hair, parted in the middle. I gave up the gardener's job at Holloway Sanatorium about this time, where I'd been since after the war, as I always wanted to be my own man.

Izzie and me shared a couple of big greenhouses and I had plans for market gardening: cabbages, lettuces, carrots, and I'm good with tomatoes. We could supply a local shop. Yesterday Izzie stood in the old north greenhouse, amongst the weeds and puddles and broken glass, pulling out the rotten wood.

'We'll make a go of this, Izzie.' I put my arm round her.

Mr Carver drove down to our cottage in April that year, Simon beside him, happy as sandboys. We had tea with thick slices of Izzie's fruitcake and talked plants.

'Your brother's a very lucky man, Izzie,' Mr Carver said. We all sat comfortably at the oak refectory table in the kitchen. He turned to Simon: 'Did you know that Mr Rhodes is quite an expert on local Surrey dialect?'

Simon looked confused.

I said, 'I'll give you a bag of *musheroons* when you go, and you be careful not to be stung by the *wapses*.'

He laughed. 'Will you teach me lots more words like that, Mr Rhodes?'

I looked into his bright eyes and brooded that I hadn't got further with my learning: the English teacher said I had a way with words. I passed for the grammar school but Mum and Dad wouldn't let me go.

Izzie and I ate on the porch that evening with a bottle of parsnip wine. The weather had broken and the sky was red in the east. Izzie had found a box of herbs and concoctions under Mum's bed, and some old papers with instructions on them. We remembered those times Mum would be out here very late, making patterns with the herbs, sometimes lighting them and chanting a strange form of words. Sounds mumbo-jumbo these days! The do-gooders would tell you it's witchcraft but really it's just the old form of religion, sometimes known as Wicca. Our family never had trouble from anyone.

Izzie was getting chilled and went in to change. She came down wearing one of mum's old dresses. It looked so natural to me, seeing her like that. I gave her a squeeze, and she kicked up her heel like a young girl.

By the May of '63 there was some order in the Carvers' garden. We'd got bedding plants and herbs, weeping figs and azaleas from Richmond Nurseries in Windlesham. Mrs C used to wander down the garden to seek me out, her shoes caressed the grass like two pretty serpents hissing. She saw me planting a row of white alyssum. 'Mug of coffee, Will?' She bent over, put it beside me with the biscuits, and her perfume rose up from her cleavage. 'Will,' she says. I know what's coming. 'Would those red ones be better in that flowerbed over there?' So I move them. 'I wonder if they do look quite right there, Will...?'

So it went on. I'd start planting and Mrs Carver was for rearranging. We got by. By the summer of '65 the garden was a picture, and all the structural work was complete. Their regular gardener was still poorly so I took over the main bulk of work. Mr Carver came on more hunched and walked rather crooked. Over the next few years many of the old houses in the village passed from families who had owned them for over a hundred years: we lost the Birchetts, the Denyers and the Worsfolds. Newcomers to the village had no roots, all new money, lots of Jew boys.

In the autumn of 1967 Izzie was feeling squashed in the back bedroom, so she took over Mum and Dad's room. It felt natural seeing her there. When she had nightmares I comforted her — I smelt the history of our family, of our neck of the woods. It was Mum's smell too, when I was a nipper before the war, and no one could imagine the changes coming. I made Izzie a special mixture of herbs from an old book of Mum's. That worked nicely and her bad dreams fled. Some nights she still got scared. 'Don't leave me just yet, Bill,' she whispered.

'You'd make someone a lovely wife, Izzie!'

She was right off the tablets from the doctor for her nerves. A few nights later we made a celebration dinner, steaming up home-made steak and kidney pudding, new potatoes, greens, carrots, peas, my special beer gravy — put back a good few bottles of pale ale too!

Then Izzie turned in. I took her up a cocoa and opened the window. She was wearing one of Mum's linen nightgowns. I'd put in a tot of Lamb's Navy Rum — we called this our 'Magic Cocoa' — and it was part of the 'treatment' for the good nights she was now having.

'That's lovely, Will,' she touched my arm. She was beautiful in the soft light.

'Good night, Mum,' I laughed.

'Good night, Dad.' She gave a gasp and hugged me.

'Good night, my sweet.' I kissed her slowly.

One morning in December '67 I turned up early at the Carvers. Frost was hard on the gate and the hinges creaked.

'I won't be bossed by your father, Simon. I won't be told who I can see.'

A plate crashed in the kitchen. The French windows in the drawing room flew open. She darted into the garden, wearing a powder-blue silk dressing-gown.

That night I talked it over with Izzie: 'It's bad what's going on at the Carvers.' The Christmas decorations in our cottage made me sadder for young Simon and Mr Carver. 'You and me must stay close, my dear girl.' Celebrations in the village were just tinsel, wishing 'Happy Christmas' to those you didn't know from Adam. On Christmas Eve the St Mary's bells played their special rounds but sounded flat and dimmed.

'That mistletoe's lovely, Will.' I held the chair as Izzie tied bunches in the front-room. I turned red holly sticks in my fingers and placed a garland in her hair. We had the first slices of our home-cured ham, pease pudding and roast potatoes. I put fresh hazel logs on the fire and after supper we sat close on the sofa and sang a favourite folk song of Dad's, 'The Wanton Wife of Castlegate': 'Oh there was a wife in Castlegate but I won't tell of her name / She is both brisk and buxom and she likes a tumbling game....'

Foxes, hares and beasts of all kinds tried to kindle warmth for the winter solstice. Newcomers knew nothing of the magic of winter, with their central heating and double-glazing. 'Shall we have a little dance, Izzie?' I put *Liberace's Christmas* on the gramophone — how Izzie loved that old homo. Who was going to have Mrs Carver as a present, I wondered, with her silk stockings and black suspenders?

I took Izzie up her magic cocoa. The embroidered bolster pane had slipped down. She made two little rabbit's ears with the sheet and wiggled her hand to make a mouth. 'You'll catch your death, Izzie.' I pulled the sheet and the blankets right around her. The wind was coming off the Hogs Back. 'You must keep warm, my girl.' I put my arm round her and took the weight off my feet. Wind hummed in the chimney and shaped stories of the old Surrey, long dead: I sensed the panting hounds as Lord de la Warr led the Surrey Union on their Boxing Day Hunt over crisp white fields. 'We don't have secrets, do we Izzie?'

'Hold me tight, Will.'

A few days later Mr Carver was chatting to me by the potting shed, smoking one of his Sullivan Powell Turkish cigarettes, his long, bony hand shaking ash over his jacket. Mrs C jingled up the path at the far side of the garden.

That evening I was feeling low and took sustenance from the root of a special fuchsia I'd planted secretly. It always perked me up. I learnt years ago, on a Home Service programme, that the voodoo leaders in Haiti, where the fuchsia was first seen by a white man in the sixteenth century, used the plant in many magic rituals. Funny, the affinity of the old ways. I pulled some of Mum's dusty books from under the bed. There was an ancient one by John Dee and many diagrams in my grandmother's hand; she was a Tizzard, straight out of Dorset and into service at Lord Stannard's in Ripley. In *Culpeper's Complete Herbal*, Mum had written a list in pencil of the herbs she valued most.

During that summer of '68 Izzie became more independent, 'Be back later, Will.' She was wearing a new flowery frock.

'Izzie, don't give away the family secrets to that old gossip!'

She was visiting Nancy Weston, a fair, big-limbed Scandinavian-looking woman, who owned the tobacconist shop, and had never married. She'd come from Brighton five years ago and bought the business. She and Izzie often went out together and by the winter they were as close as thieves. She gave Izzie a bunch of carnations one time. I cut the heads off in the night. No one said anything.

In January '69 I worked on building a rockery in the far end of the Carvers' garden. I came back late one night.

'It's lovely having a friend like you, Nancy.'

They were drinking white wine and chewing sticky doughnuts.

'You can tell me anything, Izzie, you know that,' Nancy said and gave me her cold grey-eyed look as I undid my boots. 'Izzie could do with a good woman friend, don't you think, Will?' The hairs on Nancy's strong right arm stood up as she stroked Izzie's shoulder. Izzie went quiet after Nancy left.

'No, I can manage, Will,' Izzie said as I offered to help with supper.

I stood on the porch and sipped a Mackeson. I saw deep cracks in the ground and felt a rumble from the earth like we were all going down. After our meal Izzie said, 'I may go and see Nancy; she's got some clothes she wants me to try on.' Izzie was wearing lipstick and new nylons.

February was damp, like the ghosts of the little river Bourne were breathing over us. I didn't go to the pub much these days. One evening I took Izzie up her magic cocoa, and pulled the covers nicely over her.

'That's all right, Will, I can manage. I'm tired, thank you.'

'Izzie, there's no secrets.'

'I'm very tired, Will. Goodnight.' She coloured red.

'But you've been so well these years on our concoctions.'

'Nancy says I've always been well.'

'Nancy's an interfering busybody!'

The next day Izzie returned to the back bedroom. The doctor had to give her tablets again for her bad dreams. In March I was finishing off the rockery. Mrs C swanned down the poppy path. 'Mr Carver suggested you had coffee with him in the kitchen.'

'Thank you.'

'I'm sorry to hear that Izzie is unwell at the moment.'

'She's not "unwell," Mrs Carver, just her nerves are a bit funny. Kind of you to inquire.' I cracked a willow twig.

Mr Carver was laying back on the dark-blue velvet sofa, studying the dog etchings by Cecil Aldin he loved so much.

'You mustn't listen to everything Mrs C says about me, sir, I don't mean her no harm at all, it's just...'

'She doesn't speak behind your back,' but he kept his eyes on the pictures. 'Let's look at these,' he said. He showed me plant books and turned the pages very urgent; he made me write down his order; 'There,' he said at the end and sighed.

Mr Carver died on 21 November, 1969.

In the January of 1970 the county council changed the signposts all over our district. They took away the black and white cast-iron posts, with 'Surrey' engraved in the hooped top. I know those posts had been there since 1918, my Uncle John had put them up himself. Now we've got big black and blue neon ones and you may as well be in Toytown. I suppose the newcomers can find their way home better.

There are a couple of little hillocks beyond our cottage and that winter I took to studying Mum's books there. The fissures in the earth made me afraid of sitting on the grass lest I might tumble into the darkness. But at night, if I rested my ear against the cool dew, nature's secrets entered my ears.

In January '71 Simon came into the potting shed. He was on holiday from boarding school. He was a handsome boy but something fearful burned in his eyes.

She came down with a coffee for me.

'Don't disturb Will, darling.'

She stroked the mug's rim with her finger, and put the cup down. She watched it all the time, willing me to drink. Simon followed his mother back to the house. His shoulders were hunched. There was a strain of his mother in that boy and he needed my help. The spirit of poor Mr Carver tipped coffee from the mug and I knew I should not drink. I threw it hard against the door.

One freezing evening in late February I came back to the cottage and saw Nancy in the parlour, wearing black, mannish trousers, standing beside Izzie's chair.

'Nancy's asked me to move in with her, Will.'

Nancy put her big hand on Izzie's shoulder.

'Are you well enough, Izzie? You've been on your tablets again lately?'

'Oh, make her mad, Will. Control her for ever, won't you!' Nancy combed Izzie's hair.

'You're speaking out of place, Nancy. I take care of Izzie.'

'I know what you take care of, Will Rhodes.'

I went to our herb garden and picked sage and rosemary for the roast pork. When I got back Nancy was packing Izzie's clothes.

'I'll be better when I go, Nancy says.'

'The doctor put you back on your tablets, first time for years.'

'She'll care for me lovely.'

In the spring I bought some rare fuchsias to plant in memory of Mr Carver who loved them so and was most knowledgeable. In the evenings I studied hard and made two or three herb concoctions. I sat in my favourite field near the cottage but the cracks in the earth were that wide now, and I soon returned to the kitchen, fearing they would take me down. On the table I wound yarrow stalks and other plants into five rings and put them in the various mixtures.

Later that week, on the back porch, I chanted a special form of words over the yarrow rings as I took them out of the concoctions I'd made up. Then I tied a yarrow ring to each root of a fuchsia. That evening I moved into Mum and Dad's room and felt cozier there.

On the Wednesday morning a Miss Roberts from Social Services in Guildford paid me a visit. 'Perhaps your sister would benefit from a complete absence of contact with you for a while, Mr Rhodes?' Nancy Weston must have been making trouble again. The social worker's round glasses clicked as she set them on her nose. I offered her tea but couldn't find a clean cup. 'Do you think your house is quite hygienic, Mr Rhodes?' She brushed her tweed skirt as she left.

It was a bright clear day; I took the five fuchsias down to the Carvers and planted them, saying heartfelt prayers for the spirit of that good man. White magic for Mr Carver, Simon and Izzie, and something darker for Mrs C and Nancy. I could smell Mum's breath as she whispered in my ear.

It was a cold April. I'd lost interest in the market garden and the greenhouse was littered with shards of glass from the vandals. I put my favourite fuchsia in a pot in the bedroom and my lips suckled the soft and yielding roots in the dark. I drew the curtains against the full moon and hung wild garlic over the door.

The Way

Heaving sounds, throaty coughs and barking dogs woke Alan. He rubbed his unshaved chin and realised they must be reinforcing the barricades. The canvas walls of the living space in the old army lorry, an Albion Clansman, were sticky. The cream blanket, pulled tight round his body, smelt of wood smoke. He got up and flicked on a Calor gas ring.

The red kettle soon hissed. The noticeboard was crammed: maps; eviction notice; emails of support from other travellers; potential escape routes. The chipped mug warmed his hands as he sipped sweet Camp coffee.

On the carved Indian table there was a ring of small glass beads that his partner, Moira, had made before she had moved off with their two children. He wasn't going to have them go through another eviction. The dream catcher his daughter had left for him was pinned to one of the lorry's ceiling struts. Dangling strands of thread caressed his shoulder. He tucked the contraption away in a drawer. Above the bed, his son's brightly crayoned picture of a hairy traveller holding a placard proclaiming 'No!' made him laugh.

He switched on his laptop. Emails raced onto the screen.

Squelching boots disturbed him.

'Ooh, it's Lady Muck. What's she doing here?' a male voice said.

He knew who it was. He pulled back the curtain at the other side of the lorry and gazed at the wide fields that stretched up to the Ridgeway. Last night's storm had blown itself out. Watery sunlight spread across the sky and glassy yellow light glistened through the window. The harvest had been gathered in two weeks ago but the land retained the colour of burnt gold. He had looked out at this arid country each day for two years and never before had he loved a landscape so much: the ancient rocks and stones transferred strength into his body and spirit: after twenty years on the road he didn't want to travel any more. What the hell did she want? He brushed long hair away from his fair, worn handsome face and opened the door. 'Suppose you'd better come in.'

'Then I shall.'

Someone shouted to him, 'The police have blocked off two roads — one from Streatley, the other from Ashampstead.'

'They're trying to stop the photographers getting through,' he said.

Her yellow Wellingtons were mud spattered and the green raincoat baggy. A Robin-Hood-style hat sported a pheasant feather. 'I wanted to explain.'

'Bit late.'

She came in with a rush, all parts of her small body in motion, her stick falling to the floor. He picked it up.

'Irish Hawthorn, my husband's favourite.'

'You didn't come to talk about walking sticks.'

'No, well.'

'There's time for a coffee before the police arrive.'

'Thank you.'

As the kettle burbled on the stove he looked outside. A strange thing had happened during the time he had lived here: a small path of round stones had revealed themselves across Wilcox's land, beginning at the lowest point, where the soil could be boggy, and reaching high towards the horizon in the west. On a few occasions he had seen a track, luminous in its speckled whiteness. When he had gone to investigate the path didn't seem to cohere at all.

'The kettle's whistling,' she said.

He handed her the coffee in the unchipped green dragon design cup.

'You voted against us at the parish council meeting,' he said bitterly, 'we thought you were on our side.'

'It was complicated.' She took off her hat and stroked the feather. 'It wasn't really you, but I had concerns about some of the others.'

'What can you expect?' he stirred his tea. 'It's like being a stretcher bearer at the end of a battle. You get a lot of hangers on, losers, druggies.'

'What's the war?'

'This mad world is choking to death. The technological power of late-Capitalism...'

'I never took you for a fanatic sort.'

He laughed in spite of himself. 'It's us who may be the norm soon. The rest of you won't know how to survive.'

Bunches of dried herbs, in a variety of shades and shapes, hung from the ceiling. She shut her bright eyes. 'Such a lovely smell, reminds me of my childhood.'

'Moira grew them — why did you turn against us?' He walked across to the window.

'I was forced to.'

She stood by him. 'It spoils the view, doesn't it?'

A massive red combine harvester, a new Massey Ferguson, was parked in the corner of a field.

'David Wilcox always likes to show off, but his father was quite different: known locally as Basher Wilcox, had a half-blue in boxing; that was it, Oxford. He loved the land.'

'So?'

'Did you see the partridge?' She pointed in a south-westerly direction, 'that's where my cottage is; I use as a studio. I still live at The Paddock, that old Jacobean house up the hill.'

'I won't be living anywhere soon.'

'I'm so sorry.' She dropped her stick again. 'I... life... my husband died recently, the house rattles — if you ever need boots, rainwear, all in the outhouse, I couldn't face...'

'Please.'

'I'm doing it again, putting my foot in it. You are about to be evicted, I know. I'm going to say one more thing to make you cross. How did you end up here, you seem, you'll hate this, well-born?'

' "Well-born!" – I don't have time to get philosophical with you.'

Outside, a shout: 'You can't go there!'

A tousle-haired young woman stood at Alan's open door, 'I'm from the *Reading Mercury*; I found a way through the police roadblocks. There are more travellers coming.' She pointed to a group scrambling over hedges.

'Well done,' he said, admiring her girl-guide enthusiasm.

A photographer stood at her side.

'Get on the roof if you want to,' Alan said to him, 'it's a good view from up there.'

Back inside the old lady was staring out of the window. 'He wants to buy my cottage, you see, that's the nub of it.'

'What?'

'It's in the way of David Wilcox's plans for his country sports centre.'

'So?'

'I refused, last month, well before the parish council meeting.' Tears dripped down her cheeks.

He handed her a box of tissues.

'I thought if I voted against you,' she covered her eyes. 'I'm a cowardly old woman.' She pulled two spent 12 bore cartridges from her raincoat pocket, 'that he'd leave me alone.'

Alan's mobile rang and one of his watchers on the local roads told him the police would be here in half an hour. He stood on the steps. 'Get ready,' he shouted.

He sat next to the old lady. ' "Leave you alone?" What do you mean? Who?'

It all came out. For the past two years she had enjoyed David Wilcox's charm: dinners at his house, and a visit to the Theatre Royal, Windsor. He overwhelmed her with arguments about how his country pursuits centre would be good for the community, and 'These gypsies are ruining the fabric of the village – we mustn't cave in to woolly liberal thinking.' There had been silent phone calls in the night, and a dumper truck of pigs' swill dropped on her front lawn.

The canvas roof dipped as the photographer took up position.

'Be careful,' Alan warned him.

'So I thought we had an agreement,' she continued, 'I would vote against you – he said there had been rumours in the village of someone who had a vendetta against me – and he could stop it.' An emerald ring glowed on her middle finger. 'Then he would stop badgering me about selling my cottage. I have never known such things, Alan. I agreed, but then this.' She forced the cartridges into his hand. 'Last night there were shots in my garden, the cartridges dumped on my front door step. The dogs yelped, so I got up and sent out the retrievers. He, they, got away, but...' She held up a piece of paper.

It was noisy outside and Alan went to investigate. People were organising themselves behind vehicles, picking up stones and lengths of wood. Two men were making Molotov Cocktails. 'We don't want that!' he screamed at them.

The old lady came out and stood by him. 'I was once caught up in riots in Pakistan. This will be kindergarten stuff. 'You are a good man, Alan.'

'This bill,' she thrust it into his hand, 'someone must have dropped it when the dogs frightened them.'

'What is it?' He led her inside.

'It's a diesel bill from the garage David Wilcox uses for his farm vehicles, dropped by one of his men.'

'You can't be sure.'

'On the back, look, "Just frighten her!" in a rather simple hand.'

'That was silly of them. You must tell the police, but it's too late for us.'

'I'm not going anywhere.' She stood by the window. 'I've been dreaming of the land.'

Police sirens wailed in the lane.

'I shall speak to Wilcox, and we'll have an Extraordinary Meeting of the parish council. It's not too late — and you could stay in my cottage, fair rent; I don't want to use it anymore, and your family would have somewhere.'

Two lines of police stood beyond the barricades, backed up by dogs with their handlers. On the roof the *Reading Mercury* photographer stood up to get a better view.

'They've got the fucking press here!' A policeman had forgotten to turn off his megaphone.

Ironic jeers rose up. The young women journalist made her way to the front of the barricade: 'May I have an interview with the inspector please?' There was no response and the police line stood very still, riot shields raised. A few minutes later policeman and dogs began to clamber over the barricades. The travellers picked up their weapons. Alan stood on the steps with a loudhailer and the old lady grabbed it, almost falling off the steps.

'Listen to me.' Even through the static her voice was clear. 'Get the chief constable down here. You must tell him that Lady Touchard believes an injustice has been committed.'

Noise ceased. The dogs were pulled to attention.

'There must be negotiations,' she went on.

'What the hell are you doing there, madam, Lady Touchit?' the inspector asked.

'I see you there, David. Come out from under that tree and let's talk. I think a solution may be found. I have something of yours that you may have left outside my house.'

The senior policeman said: 'Madam, this has nothing to do with you. Leave this site at once or be arrested.'

Travellers roared support for their new champion; they beat sticks against tin drums.

'I have no intention of leaving. I'm sure the press will report this matter fairly.'

There was a click as the policeman turned off his megaphone.

'No one do anything.' Alan stared at the group of anarchists. 'Move away from the barricades. No violence. Nothing.'

Beneath the tree David Wilcox was gesticulating at one of his farm workers. He walked across to the inspector.

'Get on with it,' one of the anarchists jeered, holding a Molotov cocktail above his head.

'Put that down now!' Alan raised his fist.

A blast of wind arrived from nowhere and the panting tongues of the police Alsatians flapped like flags. Exhaust smoke from the police vehicles spun in the air. Policemen relaxed their grip on their shields but stared from behind the visors of their riot helmets.

Fifteen minutes later the inspector's megaphone crackled: 'This is an unusual situation, Lady Touchard. After talking to Mr Wilcox, and with the chief constable, I am prepared to allow a discussion to take place between you, Mr Wilcox and Alan Wright, the travellers' leader.'

The crowd cheered.

Lady Touchard stood on the steps of the army lorry with Alan. They scanned the travellers for signs of disorder. The Molotov Cocktails were on the ground, the rag fuses taken out. David Wilcox climbed over the barricade and walked towards them.

My Niece, Jet Harris, and the Coalman

Gold stars on the blue-sloped ceiling of my attic bedroom glinted. I was nine and the world was fresh. I got up and inched back the curtains. Thin layers of watery ice on the window slid away as my fingers pushed them into the corners. There was snow outside, thick on the grass, flowerbeds and trees. The bottom of the sky was clouded and higher up it was blue with an orange glow.

Downstairs in the playroom Mother was baby-talking to my eighteen-month-old niece. My sister and her husband had gone to Germany for a week. I said 'Hello' to Mummy and she responded 'Good Morning' but didn't turn round.

'Can't you look at me?' I said.

'Don't be so rude.'

Suzie banged her head on the table. 'Now look what you've done.'

I slammed the door and went into the dining room where I sat in my father's place but didn't feel like breakfast. The snow had stopped and grey light covered the walls. I wondered when they would let him out of hospital.

Upstairs, I played with my Scalextric but both the Brabham and Ford Mustang needed new brushes and jerked along the track. I read more of a Hardy Boys book, *Torch Mystery*.

Half an hour later Mother shouted up, 'Simon, you need exercise.'

We all bundled up.

The roads and pavements were packed hard with ice-snow. I pulled Suzie on the toboggan to the level crossing and Mother said I was too slow, but she smiled and was happier in the cold fresh air, in her tweed jacket, old boots and woven scarf. It snowed in great swirls and we turned left into Rusham Road, then right into Alma Road.

'Jet Harris's mother lives in one of these little houses,' Mother said.

'He's one of the Shadows, isn't he, and played for Cliff Richard?'

'He's famous now... Simon, look!'

A trim man with short fair hair, blue jeans, black winklepicker shoes, jumped out of his car.

'Ga, ga.' My niece became excited when she saw Jet Harris's thin, red electric guitar, which he carried without a case.

'Darling, he's famous, and you could be if you wanted.'

'How?'

'Your little niece gets the idea, don't you, Suzie. Jet's mother used to be a daily for Madge Sutcliffe in Virginia Water. Anyone can be a star now, isn't that marvellous?'

Jet Harris strode down the alleyway at the side of his mother's house.

He turned and gave us a pop-star smile. On the other side of the tight street, Vince the coalman pushed open the two wide doors of his yard. His black shiny cap was decorated with snowflakes.

'Hello, young'un,' he said.

'Hello.'

'Got to get a few sacks to Mrs Drummond, but I won't bother to get the lorry out.'

His black ex-army boots crunched over the hard snow in the yard, and his black overalls shone as if they had been polished by coal dust. Susie began to cry and Mother said we must get home now. Vince lifted a coal sack high onto his left shoulder and lugged a smaller one at his side.

I pulled the toboggan. Vince walked beside us in the road. We reached the Alma and inside old men huddled together while their cigarettes burnt bright. Big flakes fell in the soundless day and made new layers of whiteness.

I tugged on the toboggan and the rope snapped. 'No,' Suzie said, 'too rough, rough.' She cried.

'Take more care, Simon.'

Would they let my father out of hospital soon?

Vince tied the rope together. His gold wedding ring glowed.

'I'll help you, Vince?'

'Are you allowed?' He winked at Mother.

She smiled back. His teeth were bright against the coal smudges on his cheeks. I picked up the little sack and followed him. Mrs Drummond lived far up Hurst Lane in a cottage. Snow blew round us. The pavements, cars and houses became a wilderness. 'I'm coming, Vince.'

We made crunchy new tracks as we disappeared into the blurry white.

After Father's Funeral

He had been ill for so long that it was not like losing a whole father. In the weeks before he died I read *The Times* to him in the cottage hospital and began to like him again; I knew that he loved me.

I remember the crematorium: I was forced to wear my suit; when I got out of the big funeral car I stepped in a puddle. The area had been tarmaced and looked like a motorway service station. It was a wet grey day. Mother stood beneath a neat black umbrella and dipped her head so that the fringed hat was at the most flattering angle on her pretty painted face. She wore a grey Jaeger two-piece suit, and black Bally shoes.

It was a modern chapel with light-coloured pews like balsa wood; about forty people huddled towards the front. The vicar, who did not know my father, mentioned 'Geoffrey's contribution in the war' and 'his committed work for the Rotary Club'. Mother held a lace handkerchief to her eyes. My father's oak coffin with brass handles moved easily into the flames.

After the funeral there was a gathering at The Red Lion. Mother greeted everyone warmly, and the men especially comforted her with kind words. People treated me as if I had lost a rugby match or failed an exam and needed cheering up. We had taken over the main bar. There was plenty of food and drink and two open coal fires glowed.

Mother smiled, fluttered her eyelids, and glanced at her watch when she thought no one was looking. She was expecting Karl Schmidt. She drank more gin and tonics, flushed a little, took me aside and said, 'I need love; you must understand.'

I picked up my half pint of cider from the bar and walked into the car park. Roads at this roundabout went off in four directions. She followed me: 'You must be nice to him, for my sake. Please, darling.' I moved away but she grabbed my arm. I yanked free.

'You little shit!' Her lips stretched downwards.

I went inside. At the bar, John Wiley, who owned the Ferrari garage, put his arm round my shoulder. 'I think he should be allowed another half pint of cider, don't you, landlord?'

I could see mother fidgeting outside. Then Schmidt's Saab turned into the entrance. She rushed over. He got out. They hugged.

I thanked John for the cider and took a deep gulp.

Susanna at Maidenhead

Her parents' bed was wide and silky. Susanna hopped over to the record player and put on 'Lola' by the Kinks. We always listened to that first. She undid her white blouse: 'How shall we do it today, Simon?'

After, we stretched and giggled. Fitz was coming round this evening, worse luck. The two flights of stairs of the scruffy Victorian house vibrated with dust as I ran down. The Blue Mountain coffee was hidden in its usual place in the breakfast room. Soon the percolator bubbled and Atomic Rooster's 'Devil's Answer' screamed from the radio. I bet Susanna it would be number one by the end of 1971. At the top of their long garden the July sun shot rays onto the chrome of my new BSA Lightning 650. I bought it with the money my father left me. I took up two mugs of coffee and a packet of milk-chocolate digestive biscuits.

'Put it there,' she said.

Three sets of eyes and mascara brushes stared out from the three-mirrored dressing-table. A photo of her father glowered: Dr Danzell was from Trinidad, half-Indian and looked like Rohan Kanhai. He had once been a psychiatrist in Yorkshire, but there had been problems and he now worked as a drugs consultant for a pharmaceutical firm in Slough. Her mother was from Somerset. They had gone to Weston for the weekend with Susanna's sister and brother.

'What you got?' Susanna asked.

'Black. Very fresh.' I inhaled slowly.

We were both at the Windsor Tutorial College for deviants and dropouts and you could get anything. We passed the joint back and forth. The last few days had been heavy, and nothing had gone right. But it was the beginning of the summer holidays. We had the weekend to ourselves, except for Fitz. Susanna showered and I cleaned my bike.

My mother had gone racing to Newmarket with her bouffant-thatch Italian arsehole of a boyfriend. She thought he was a trainer. Last week I told Hair-Perm that a friend of mine had seen him serving in the bar at Ascot racecourse. 'You leetle sheet, you leetle sheet.' Mother walked in and he backed off.

At six the front-door bell tinkled.

'Osgood, Osgood, Chelsea Shed, Chelsea Shed.'

'Hello Fitz,' I said.

'Simon.'

He swayed with his Chelsea scarf in both hands above his skinhead haircut. I supported Spurs but Fitz put me off football.

'Come in.'

His cold face smiled. His long thin body was set off by well-polished black Doc Martens boots, too-short jeans, a Ben Sherman red-check shirt and braces. His complexion was grey and his teeth bright. His father was a dentist but Fitz behaved like a working-class hero of the football terraces. He used to talk about sea fishing with his father, and the special bacon, mayonnaise and curry powder sandwiches they ate in their boat off Hastings. He never mentioned that anymore. Fitz and Susanna were 'best friends' and to get her at weekends I often had to put up with him. 'He understands me,' she said. He was at our college and we were taking A Levels next year.

'Fitz is here.'

She came down in a big white towel. 'Ello darlin'.' She hugged him and returned upstairs.

We sat in the breakfast room but didn't talk. A few minutes later Susanna came in wearing a slinky Indian print red-patterned skirt, a white top and brown-leather sandals. Fitz's tight mouth uncurled as his eyes followed her.

'Let's make a proper supper,' I said, 'I'll get stuff from the garden.'

They laughed because they liked crap food. Fitz took out a bottle of Strongbow from his carrier bag and filled glasses for each of us. 'And....' He made a conjuror's gesture and lay pills on the palm of his hand.

'Not speed,' I moaned.

'You're no fun,' Susanna said. 'It always clears my head. Fitz understands.' She put a Dexie in her mouth.

'Hippies don't like to feel alive, do they, man.'

'Piss off.'

His thumb rubbed the shoulder of my red Paisley shirt.

'But I'm a hippy sort of girl,' she simpered.

'You're different. Go on, have another.'

She stuck out her tongue at me and took a second. Fitz gobbled several. I walked out.

The smell of frying beef burgers and onions hissed up the garden path. I picked lettuces and tomatoes, washed them, made a salad and poured over Heinz French dressing. Fitz flipped burgers onto our plates.

'This is food for foot-ballers, foot-ballers'.... His voice warbled and bovver boots crashed around as he danced.

We took our plates into the breakfast room and sat in the gloom. Fitz shoved his burger and fried onions into a bap, squeezed the tomato sauce bottle, and red mush splattered across the table. They laughed hysterically.

'You're no fun,' Susanna looked at me.

Gunge dribbled down Fitz's chin.

'I love you Fitz because you never talk about poetry.'

I was the only one who ate the salad.

'And you don't have only one thing in your mind.' Her cleavage pointed at him.

I did the washing up.

They came into the kitchen arm in arm. Fitz turned to me. 'Have you seen my impersonation of Ted Heath?' He used his braces and white teeth very well. Then he did one of Tommy Cooper. His dilated eyes were pin pricks.

'More fun...Chelsea...More fun...Chelsea....' He ran white powder along the work surface. 'It's Billy Whizz, powder form!'

'No more speed, Fitz,' I said.

He snorted it up. 'Come on, Suze. Let's show hippy boy what a good time is.'

'I think we've had enough, Fitz. I want you to see my latest design.' She went upstairs.

He poured cider until it dribbled over the rim of my glass.

'Stop, Fitz.'

'Piss off, Spurs scum.'

I managed to get him out to the patio. She returned with two pairs of Doc Martens shoes sprayed in different colours and with multicoloured laces.

'Sit down and take your boots off,' she said.

Susanna was crazy about shoes and a college in Switzerland was going to give her a scholarship to study shoe design.

'I'll try the phantasmagoric pair, man,' Fitz said and his lip twitched. 'Don't think they'll catch on.'

They were amazing. He jigged across the patio and up the path into the vegetable garden, 'We are the Chelsea shed boys, we are the boys to watch....' He crashed on to an old glass cloche, smashing it to bits. The next-door neighbour, on a ladder clipping his hedge, stared down. The sun slipped behind the garage. Susanna led Fitz into the sitting room and we gave him coffee. He paced round the sofa cracking his knuckles.

I set up a game of Monopoly on the floor. Fitz was the racing car, I was the top hat, and Susanna the shoe. After seven or eight turns Fitz already had Bond Street and Regent Street. 'Well done, Fitz,' we said. By ten he was drunk on cider, which was better, and the speed was wearing off.

'I don't hate you, Simon, just...'

'That's okay, Fitz.'

Susanna put her arms round him. 'I'm always your friend, always.'

An hour later we tucked him up on the sofa with blankets and went upstairs.

'Next time don't be so bloody stupid,' I said.

'Who said there'd be a next time for you?'

'Shut up.'

We went to bed; she burst into tears and held me, but soon turned away and fell asleep. As we lay on separate sides I saw my mother in bed with her horrible new boyfriend. I put my head close to Susanna's beautiful face, her hands curled up like the paws of a cat, and I wanted to love her so much. She had to sleep with the thick dark curtains drawn tight. As they shivered in the breeze I saw my father's coffin going down the conveyor belt through curtains just like that. I got up to let in a strip of light. A half moon lit the low hills that were real country all the way to Marlow. They were planning to build an estate of new 'Executive' houses.

'No, no!' Susanna screamed.

Fitz stood over us in a Chelsea bobble hat and no clothes.

'You said last time we could do it together, do it together.'

His face was frantic with twitching. He had taken more speed.

'She loves me too, bastard; last week she snogged me.'

I sat upright.

'We are the Chelsea boot boys...Lofty is our hero...' The pus spots on his back were purple as he jumped on the bed between us.

'Please, Fitz — please.' She tugged the sheet.

He pushed his toes into the mattress.

'No, Fitz!'

She rolled naked out of bed and into the corridor and then came back in a dressing gown. I put on my trousers.

'You snogged me last week, and pretty boy should know that.'

'Stop it, Fitz, please, please.' She sobbed.

He lay flat on the bed and then jerked upright.

I picked up her dusty hockey stick.

'Spurs have won...Chelsea retreat...Chelsea retreat...'

He crashed his way downstairs.

'He's a maniac, Susanna. If you want him, then you won't have me.'

I wedged a chair behind the door and we got into bed.

Early next morning I peered into the sitting room. A rod of light came through the curtain's gap and lit up the breastplate of the cast-iron Duke of Wellington — Dr Danzell's prized collection of model soldiers from the Napoleonic Wars! — scattered like casualties on the floor. Thick blankets made an igloo over the sofa.

'Tea, Fitz?'

His fingers uncurled.

'Fitz. Tea?'

Drops of blood fell on his hand.

'Fitz!'

I pulled off the blankets: fresh blood and clotted blood from thin slashes up his arm. 'Oh, Fitz.' I turned him over. He had cut the spots on his back with a penknife. 'Don't care,' he said, 'Don't care.' He hid his head in the pillow.

'Susanna! Susanna!'

She ran down. 'God, what have I done?'

'Just help,' I said.

She got bandages, Dettol, a bowl of warm water, a flannel, and cleaned him up. I folded his penknife and took it away. Susanna made him some Heinz oxtail soup and held his hands round the mug as he sipped. She tiptoed into the corridor and summoned me with her finger.

'I'm going to call Fitz's father.' She picked up the phone and had an abrupt conversation.

Then Susanna and I went into the garden. An hour later his father turned up, 'What have you done with my son?' He glowered on the doorstep, tall and paunched in his V-neck Pringle golf jumper.

'He brought the drugs...the speed,' I said.

'Don't talk to me like that. It's disgraceful what you get up to.' Light bounced off his big square glasses.

'You ran off with your dental nurse.' Susanna smiled at him.

He flushed and pushed past us. Ten minutes later Fitz followed him out, his head down.

'You haven't heard the end of this.' He slammed the driver's door.

'Sort out your own family first,' Susanna shouted.

We washed the blankets and cleaned up. A few bloodstains did not come out of the sofa. Then we put the soldiers away into their velvet display case. One of the foot soldiers had a snapped bayonet.

I left in the late afternoon and rode home slowly.

Bouffant features was in the hall practising putting with my father's green umbrella.

'Hello, Simon; one day I take you and your mother to Italy, to Rome, my town.'

'That's a very old umbrella. Do you mind putting it back?'

'Oh, the hippy is cross.' He putted a golf ball hard along the corridor.

'Put it back, please.'

'We will become friends, but your mother she needs a friend too.' He smiled. 'Mummy will be back soon.' He putted another golf ball.

I was as tall but he was thickset with dangerous hands. I picked up my cricket bat from the bottom of the stairs and smashed it sideways against his wrist.

'Owh! No, no.'

I hit the bat across his shoulder blades. 'Don't bother my mother again. Fuck off.'

'I'll tell her, I'll tell her; you will be in such trouble. Silly little boy.'

He rushed out of the front door.

His black Lancia 2000 screeched up the drive. I kissed my father's umbrella.

Probably no girlfriend and perhaps no mother. Half an hour later she came in with bags of shopping and I told her the lot. 'Rather an extreme thing to do, darling.' She sighed. 'I was lonely, and he was attractive, but actually rather dull after your father.'

'So why even go out with him — for three months?'

'I wasn't sure how to break it off, as I haven't done that since I was young, and in those days I was quite good at it.'

We had tea and cakes at the breakfast table.

'He was such a yob,' I said.

'I thought you were the socialist?' She frowned. 'Last week I found him looking in my handbag, for a cigarette he said.' She got up and hugged me. 'I know I've been a terrible mother recently, but I love you. Alfredo told me he owned a race horse, but he only had a share, a small one, just the tail I imagine.'

She poured herself a sherry and said that Mr Blunden, head of the Windsor Tutorial College, had phoned. He hated me. He suggested it may be better if I left. 'Sour little Methodist,' she said. 'They love cocking-a-snoop at other people's "sins" — gives them orgasms.'

'Mother!'

Smoked salmon came off in chunks as she cut. 'Can't do it like your father.' I made scrambled eggs, the way Pa taught me. We ate on the patio and drank white burgundy.

A warm breeze blew down the twilit path and whistled through the torn cricket net.

She told me that Uncle Lawrence, who had a farm in Herefordshire, suggested I stay for a month, now. 'At the end of the summer go to that crammer in Oxford for a year. We'll find you somewhere nice to stay.'

'I want to, yes.'

'Look at this.' She handed me a photograph of Lawrence's girls, Clare and Natalia, who were sixteen and eighteen. 'They liked the one I sent of you too. But don't get sex mad.'

'Unlike you.'

Later, Susanna phoned. Her mother was taking her to Weston for a few weeks. I was not allowed to see her and Dr Danzell was going to phone Ma later. 'I need you,' she sobbed as she put down the phone. Uncle Lawrence first taught me to shoot and I longed to sit in a field at dawn to bag a rabbit or hare.

Early the next morning I polished the Lightning and checked the map. After breakfast Ma helped me secure my rucksack to the rear carrier. I took a detour past Susanna's house, picked up the A40 at Marlow and sang James Taylor's 'Sweet Baby James'. I only stopped for petrol and eventually reached the Green Man pub near Mansell Lacy. I drank scrumpy in the garden as cabbage whites and red admirals skimmed the hedges.

I set off and steam-engine clouds chuffed beneath the big sun. Wheat and horse smells ripened the air. A dead branch from an elm hung across the road. In my terrible dream last night Fitz had been screaming in a block of ice. I was paralyzed and could not help him. I slowed to 30 mph. My father's bony hand touched mine, and I cried. 'Sorry Fitz. Goodbye Susanna.' Blue sky rimmed the hills. The Lightning roared as I touched 4000 revs in third. Sun sparked on the chrome as I raced through the S-shaped bend.

Very Wet Jam Sandwiches

Last day at my school. I was going to prep school next term and had Rice Crispies for breakfast. I tied my tie myself because Daddy taught me how.

Mummy zoomed her yellow Triumph Herald out of the garage and put the hood down. I jumped into the front seat, and plimsolls tied to my satchel knocked me on the ears.

We whizzed along past Great Fosters Hotel, then to Holloway Sanatorium and turned right at the traffic lights in Virginia Water. My school was on the Wentworth Estate. I looked at the badge on my blazer: 'Very Wet Jam Sandwiches', I said. The badge was V.W.J.S., which was Virginia Water Junior School. When Mummy dropped me off she said, 'Don't bite your lip.'

I ran into school for lessons and sat next to my best friend Giles. Then we had milk-break. A lot of my friends were leaving too, Ti to Papplewick and Rory to St Piran's. Giles was going to be a choirboy at St George's Chapel and wear long skirts. I didn't know where the girls were going. I told Giles a rude joke about monkeys farting.

We had more lessons, then lunch — fish pie and peas, then shortbread and custard for pudding. I was in the old dining room where the senior boys and girls sat with the headteacher, Miss Fish. In the shiny mahogany table I saw Giles making faces at me. Miss Fish said, 'I remember when your big sister and brother were here, Simon; how quickly time goes.'

Then we had games. The boys ran round the grass square in front of the gym. Giles climbed up a tree. The girls skipped and sang songs. Then we had art, and cut pictures out of newspapers.

After this we had Special Assembly in the gym. Everyone was noisy until Miss Fish walked down the middle of the aisle. She stood on the stage and her hair and face were white and her bones were wobbly like Plasticine. She said good luck to everyone going to new schools. We sang 'For I am Fearfully and Wonderfully Made' and Miss Fish's version of 'Tomorrow will be my Dancing Day'. The leaving children walked on stage and Miss Fish shook our hands.

The little children went home. The older ones stayed.

Behind the gym I said goodbye to some of the girls who were playing horses, Caroline and Claire, Suzie and Jenny. I didn't think they were proper friends before but I was going to miss them.

I got my blazer and satchel off my peg. Mummy walked up the stone steps and spoke to Miss Fish, who stroked my cap. She said I'd win lots of races at prep school and be very good at cricket and write interesting stories and do come back and see her. Miss Fish believed in music, dancing and poetry. 'Too much,' Daddy used to say. Last week we all recited a poem. Now Miss Fish smiled at me and said, 'You did it beautifully: may I hear just the first verse again?'

I coughed:

> 'My mother groan'd! my father wept,
> Into the dangerous world I leapt:
> Helpless, naked, piping loud:
> Like a fiend hid in a cloud.'

Miss Fish hugged me. 'What a lovely little fiend!'

London

Cobblers for the Revolution!

I read a bit out loud each morning to inspire me. Ivan Illich is my new guru: 'Vehicles have created more distances than they helped to create.' He wrote that in *Tools for Conviviality.* If I'm still down I roll a little number, always does the trick.

Traffic pounds above my head. And the Big-Brother helicopter is always in the sky, charting the street life of Hackney. 'Down the stairs and down the years', that's how I feel as I step into my basement shoemaker's workshop. The world is going mad but I feel safe in my bunker. There's an ancient sense of permanence here (the house was built at the time of the Napoleonic Wars).

The green revolution could be here now if everyone made their own shoes and if we only travelled as far as our shoe leather would allow. It would bring us back to our roots and give us time. As Illich says: 'Development must be in terms of low and not high energy use'.

I like sitting at my bench, picking away with my cobbler's awl, threading and stitching, making handmade shoes for the wealthy – these Oxford brogues are for an old customer. Those rich gits don't deserve such perfection, and I wonder how much they appreciate it.

Mind you, it's just as bad that most of Hackney is walking around in mass-produced trainers, all sweatiness and petro-chemicals. Then they chuck them away, never nurtured, never loved. Worse than that, lots of those people recycle tins and bottles with fervour, and buy their organic carrots, but don't realise that if they made their own shoes, and saw the limits of their walking as the limits of their world, a new sense of community would begin

I made a poster for my wall, you guessed it, a slogan from my guru:

TRANSPORTATION BEYOND BICYCLE SPEEDS DEMANDS POWER INPUTS FROM THE ENVIRONMENT

Right on, Ivan! Those speeds are destroying our pleasure and our planet. Let's all slow down. I'm going on a bit; my sister is always telling me that. But when you live in a world that is crazy but pretends it's sane, then the only way to be truly sane is not to be afraid to be crazy! I was trying to get that across to a girl – well, she was about thirty, at a party last week. I admit it probably wasn't the best chat-up line. Didn't get anywhere. Pity, she was very fit, as they say these days.

A good shoe should last at least fifteen years. A shoe is like a history lesson, but all the kids now live in a vacuum. They connect to nothing. Jesus, I sound like a sad old git. Here's an example: a party last week, at the top of the Samuel Pepys, the pub attached to the Hackney Empire. There was crap music coming out of the crap speakers; Big Screens were everywhere, showing a baseball match, then twenty-twenty cricket where none of the players looked like cricketers. There was no English draught beer on tap; it was mostly lagers from American and Poland and Holland, with silly names and daft prices. There should have been a local band in the corner. But there never is. No one has roots. I feel a whole philosophy coming on!

Everywhere, buses, cars, motorbikes, emergency vehicles. All those planes scarring the sky. The planet is dying. Tapping away at the shoes on my bench, turning, kneading, reading the stresses and strains of the leather, makes me still. Shoes are my prayer books, my litany. If I believed in God I'd be a shoe-making monk. Give up the obsession with money and travel. As always, Ivan has a phrase for it: 'Joyful Renunciation'.

I love the history of footwear: 'Wellington', that was a good boot, though there were some shite ones around in those days — the soldiers suffered from their job-lot boots.

I was born in this house: Dad was a factory inspector, Mum a district nurse. I went to an old-fashioned grammar school, then did the hippy thing, bummed in Spain for a year. After that a degree in philosophy at Swansea, then Cordwainers for shoemaking. If you were born in Hackney everyone thinks you must be a yob. Actually, I taught in a school before getting into shoes.

My parents are dead now, buried near Worthing, where they had a bungalow. Me and my sister, Lucy, split up the house: she's in the top; I've got the bottom two floors.

Life's all right. I used to be in a local rock group, used to be married, but I was more in love with my shoes — Patsy my wife went off with her acupuncturist. We got married too young. They're living in Bristol, two kids.

The smell of good leather matures, becomes alive under your fingers. Connecting the shoe together — the welt and throat and top edge, the waist and the sole — until you have made something as complete as a person, and less argumentative. No one thinks about shoes now, what they are, or what they should do. The trainer-footed world has turned its back on this inheritance that could save it.

I must put on a jumper. November is here. Hackney begins to feels cleaner and the basement older. The ghosts in this house prefer the softness of autumn, as if summer bleaches them out of existence.

I love the beauty of boots. I collect them. Those Nazi jackboots are always at the top of the stairs. They're authentic. When I imagine them, pounding down on their heavy soles, they remind me of the fascist state under the surface of things. The shoes may be softer now, and the surveillance more subtle, but it means the same thing — the state can get you when it wants.

Consider marching boots, well, it's a whole way of telling history: the places these boots have trodden, the routes they took, the army cobblers who kept the boots together. Soldiers always had the worst shoes, the ankle boots: the officers had the top boots. In the First World War it was the soldiers who suffered from trench foot, water and mud squelching through the lace holes. Of course the British army boot came out of the Blucher boot.

Cavalry boots are the most beautiful, with their bucket tops, Royalist fashion. I made a pair in college, still got them, half-way up the stairs; Cromwell's people knew a bit about boots too, and the Americans, credit where credit is due: those cowboy boots at the bottom of the stairs, amazing tooling, superb leather. I bought those ten years ago from a bootmaker in Forth Worth, Texas.

If proper leather shoes and boots were brought back, the level of consciousness would rise; leather footwear enhances our connectedness because people talk to each other as they walk. Ban superstores; ban trainers; stop fast movement. You think that's mad? Not as crazy as what goes on up there, is it?

Anyway, I'm off to Budapest on a cheap flight for a long weekend with an old mate. Don't look at me — life's full of contradictions.

Madame Sossi

I was doing a little shopping in Berwick Street market. Bobby, who sells exotic fruits, called out, 'Madame Sossi, where's that blonde bombshell you promised me?'

'Be patient,' I said, 'wait for Jupiter to enter Capricorn next week; that'll do the trick.'

Scallops for my supper tonight. Of course, I'm long retired, though I still do a few séances for favoured clients, but it's only pocket money. I'm well provided for.

Last week, who should I see in the mirror but Dylan, Dylan Thomas. He's always sober these days, radiant: 'Hello, my petalled rosebud' − what a voice. 'How is my angel of the eternal valleys?' Poor Dylan, who was up here in January 1953. I was at my peak then, 'Mademoiselle Sossi Predicts' had just begun in the *Daily Sketch*; I had a lovely figure, auburn hair, long Diana Dors dresses, a bust that hypnotized. I said to Dylan, when we came back from dinner at the Eiffel Tower, 'Don't go to America, Dylan, don't go!' He roared, 'Will it be my ruin, you mermaid of the deeps?' His hands lurched round me, 'Give me the strength, you lissom temptress.'

I never...with Dylan. You wouldn't have known where he'd been. He had a place in Redcliffe Street then, Earls Court, but he stayed with anyone who would accommodate him, and many did. Poor Dylan. I couldn't sleep while he was in America. My calling is not an easy one.

I was born in Ladbroke Grove in 1930, if you can believe it, and 'ruined' in 1945 on a summer's day in a boat on the Thames at Cookham. It was the making of me. My mother, Betty Turpin, was red with rage: 'You bloody trollop, who you been with?' I licked my lips.

On the boat with Luigi I saw an aura round his head like flowing silk scarves. I instinctively understood his whole personality. I could read auras. I had been touched by the gift. Luigi encouraged my calling. He had a revue bar in Brewer Street and gave me a job as a receptionist, as well as finding me a flat at the top of a house near Golden Square. The mirror is going misty, always a sign I'll be visited later. I moved in to Golden Square on 17 April 1946.

There was an old medium and astrologer living in Lexington Street, Miss Veronica Hanson, who had been a friend of Annie Besant. I'll put those scallops in the frying-pan, with a little oil, lemon, parsley. I studied with Miss Veronica for two years. One day she said, 'You need a name, darling – "Rosie Turpin" lacks refinement perhaps? – and El-o-Cu-Tion lessons – works bloody wonders for business.' Luigi arranged for Sybil Merchant to give me voice lessons.

I love the smell of scallops cooking, and the colour, like jewels of the sea. Luigi was so kind and I called myself 'Mademoiselle Sossi' (It was the *Daily Sketch* that introduced the 'Madame'). He was Luigi Rossi but his wife would have been unhappy if I'd called myself 'Rossi'. One of my early clients, a Polish cavalry officer, used to say to me, 'My special angel, my darling, you're so saucy, saucy,' which sounded like 'sossi'. So Sossi it was.

My voice became more refined and it was marvellous not sounding like mother. But she found out where I was living, and one evening she waited till Luigi arrived and then, kicking and screaming, she jumped on him. It was bad for business.

Darling Luigi had troubles with the taxman and a gang of Soho Maltese thugs – so he went home to Sicily with his wife and children. That was in January 1947. I never heard from him again. There have been no sightings from the other side.

These scallops are gorgeous, with a little green salad, rye bread. Soho is not what it was though – a lot of young men with firm bottoms and girls with badly applied make-up. As my friend Don Lawson used to say, 'They're just designer bohos, sweetie.' I won't bother with the curlers tonight.

One evening, after the war, December 1948, mother stood drunk outside my flat for three hours. I pretended I wasn't in. I decided to break all links with her. She was shouting horrible things about poor Luigi, and what a slut I was. I'd had enough. The next morning an old acquaintance gave me an introduction to a disciple of Aleister Crowley, and in January 1949 I travelled into deepest Surrey to meet Mr Crowley's protégé. I handed him a fee and a brooch of mother's that she'd given me years ago. We went into the woods and in a potent ceremony involving a well-built naked warlock and four chanting bare-breasted young witches a curse was placed on mother. I felt a wonderful sense of relief.

On 21 February 1949 a handsome policeman came to my flat and told me that mother had dropped dead waiting for the 43 bus. They found my address in her handbag. I could have kissed him; actually, I did.

It's lovely lying in bed, watching telly. I'm never lonely. Jeffrey Bernard still visits, 'Hello, lover, time for a vodka?' – and can he drink vodka! I hope you're happy on the astral plane, Jeffrey. He gave me a tip last week, 'Running Wild', in the 2.30 at Catterick – came in last. Some things never change.

I think I'll go to sleep in a minute. So nice to be here for the start of the new millennium, and very exciting, astrologically. General de Gaulle loved Soho, virtually set up his headquarters at the French Pub – a most attractive man considering he was so ugly. I did his astrological chart – but I mustn't go into that – I'm still bound by the Official Secrets Act.

I love these soft pillows. Never economize on pillows. And duck feather duvets, what an invention! I never married, not that I was short of offers. It's funny being so popular at my age.

Tricks

It's handy for the punters. Six months now, top-floor flat, King's Cross, council. In the afternoon I smoke a couple of joints. Afghani, only the best. Then I float over King's Cross in cotton-wool clouds. There's a lot of funny things coming at me, ain't there? From all over London they move towards me, behind the backs of their wives or girlfriends or boyfriends, or just because they're sad old gits.

My old mate, Lania, only eighteen, light-skinned black girl, tall, beautiful, keeps herself clean, knows all the tricks. Really, she's a witch, a white witch, and soon she's going to set up her own coven in Wales. She lives next door. She did my Tarot the other day. At the end I held her hands, which were shaking. I fancied her like mad.

We'd had a couple of E's at my place. Both having a night off. Sitting on the floor, very relaxed, gone midnight. She set the cards out, turned over the one that was me — The Hanged Man — and we both felt funny.

But I'm two Kennys, see: the cute blond boy who does stuff with the punters and the other who wanders over London, like on the astral plain. I do it like this: I focus my attention on the long mirror in the corner of the bedroom; my body goes misty, I slip through, and away. Leave the other Kenny to his business. He's very good. But the real Kenny travels. Through time barriers. Met Jack the Ripper the other day, off Brick Lane. I've been born before.

When the business is over, I come back through the mirror, smile at the punter, put the money away safe — loads of thieving scum in these flats.

It's the first of November today; a warm red glow in the sky, like the world is trying to hold on to summer.

Hito's coming at 7. Over on a business trip from Tokyo.

'Kenny,' one of my foster dads said to me, 'you'll either do great things, or go to the devil in a big way.'

I never got properly adopted, see. Caused my carers lots of bother. Lania's mum was a junkie and on the game to support herself. You'd be surprised how many kids there are like us. I felt this pang under my heart and we both burst into tears.

'Is this love, Kenny?' Lania giggled.

Can you imagine me and Lania settling down in Romford, having kids and going to parents' evenings? If you think someone loves you they go away. I'm all right like this, but I'd like to do it with a girl again.

You could say I slipped into this line of work. I'm only eighteen, won't have my looks for ever. Got a steady client base, no riff-raff. No trouble with pimps neither. You could say I'm in private practice. Last time Hito was over, it must have been July, he showed me a photo of his wife and two teenage daughters, near an old volcano in Japan. Cute girls. I got bobbed and highlighted yesterday at Tommy Guns in Soho.

Hito will be here any minute. I checked myself in the mirror.

The black metal box with my savings was beneath the floorboards under my bed. I counted it. Very nice for a rainy day. Wouldn't mind sharing it with Lania though.

I dressed: white chinos, black French Connection T-shirt, new snakeskin-look Chelsea boots. The mirror became milky and I'm almost the other side, looking at Kenny. Past the old gasworks, up to the Angel, Rosebery Avenue, Gray's Inn Road. I shook my head, gripped the mirror and dried my sweat. Where was I? My body materialized, ready for work.

'Hello Kito,' I said.

I took him into the living room. He's wearing his dark-blue Burberry, regulation Nikon strapped round his shoulders. I slipped his raincoat on to a hanger and put it behind the door.

His dark-grey suit — Boss, I think — was too tight, and he had on a crappy tie, blue with smudges of red diamonds. And dark-brown English brogues — he's very proud of them, Church's. His hair was grey at the temples. That's what happened when you led a double life — the stress, you naughty boy.

He took off his square, gold-rimmed glasses and smiled, his tongue oozing from his mouth. His teeth were white and he never had bad breath. His shiny burgundy briefcase rested on the small table. He rubbed a mark off the side. Then he lined up the numbers on the barrels of his brass locks, flicked open the top and handed me a brown package.

'Thanks, Kito.' I pulled off the brown paper and gave him a juicy smile.

It's *Oliver Twist*, a Folio Society edition. I've got seven Folio Dickens's now.

'Please, you Oliver Twist today. Get ready. I am Fagin.'

The briefcase clicked shut and he went to the bathroom.

In the bedroom I put on Victorian-rag clothes, smudges of mascara.

He walked up behind me in his red wig, and a tattered, brown-checked overcoat, red spotty handkerchief, green corduroy trousers, black Victorian lace-up boots.

'Where do you get your gear, Kito?'

He put a scruffy tan top hat on his head, checked the angle in the mirror.

'Stand still!' he commanded.

Don't suppose his daughters know their dad fancied Victorian waifs and strays.

A long cane whizzed in his hand; the same one he used last time when he was Wackford Squeers from *Nicholas Nickleby*. Quite a literary education on the game.

'Oliver been naughty boy!'

I stared at the mirror. Quick! Quick! From the other side of the milky-white mirror I listened to the professional Kenny: 'Mr Fagin, no, please, oh, Mr Fagin....'

Stairs at 29 Mehetabel Road

The layers of paint on the stairs of our 1863 Hackney terrace house strip off to reveal an untold history. Listen: heavy feet, soft feet, children's skipping feet, down-at-heel heavy boots of the railway-worker, bare feet, Wellington boots. This secret populace, echoing from a cave, make underground music. On reaching the basement they shuffle into communion. As I work through the night sounds become tangible things: the rustle of crinoline, a turning mangle, a gas-lamp hissing. The babble from outside – languages, sirens, quarrels, dogs, trolleys, lovers' tiffs – fade. Faces appear: from the 1871 census, the umbrella maker, the railway worker, the shoe maker. From the 1901 census I can see the paint-mixer, who must have worked at the local paint factory, at the end of our road until the 1950s.

I rub the last steps in the basement with Danish oil. The steps glow. Lines from old songs rise, each one in a different voice: 'March right on to the end of the road...' 'Daisy, Daisy, give me your answer do...' 'My old man's a dustman....'

I see one ghost clearly. Martha, I call her. She is here now, dressed in brown, in her early fifties, a serious look, dark hair in a bun, standing on the mezzanine level outside the shower room.

She moves the oil lamp back and forth, observing the congregation.

Her Finest Hour

'Doris, if I want to lie in bed till 11 and suck chocolates, then I will.'

I'm ninety-one, and it was dreary outside — September in Hackney don't exactly set the heart on fire. My Doris is sixty-one, lovely girl. You might laugh! She's ever so good to me.

I live alone in a nice house in Mehetabel Road, rent protected, bit damp but I don't mind that. Charlie died ten years ago; his chest got to him. He wouldn't give up his pipe. We were so happy. Very nice neighbours here. All middle class these days with no net curtains and the women in baggy rags! Never mind. They have lovely street parties.

Doris lives in Southend; her Ron was a postman who got into the administrative side, done very well. Now he wins prizes for his chrysanthemums. I'm always welcome there.

I will have one more chocolate caramel before I get up.

My grandson, Tommy, had trials for Leyton Orient and West Ham; he's a goalie. Then he settled down as a plumber. Works for the Water Board in Chingford. Tommy has two boys, Duncan, fourteen, and Billy, ten. I love being a great-grandmother. The family often has me over for Sundays. The weather is beginning to turn — I know in my bones when they start getting tight, like they need oiling.

The lovely tree in the pavement outside my house — it's a Fernleaf Maple — has cut-edged leaves that turn dark red in autumn. I never used to know its name and one day I asked the young architect next door. Do you know he consulted a tree book and the next day wrote it down on a posh card from the Tate Gallery with a picture of a tree on it.

I've got a Teasmade by my bed. Could be the Ritz!

Anyway, two nights ago I was in my bed and this young architect walked up the steps next door and he was dressed up to the nines – as a woman! – with a black tight skirt, seams up his stockings, platinum-blonde hair. The first time I saw him a few weeks before, I said to myself, my eye he's got himself a sexy one there. Then I wondered if it was a lady of the night, just visiting like. But when I saw him under the neon lights I recognised his walk and his features.

Nothing shocks you when you've been through the war in Hackney. I worked in the docks near Milwall as charwoman for a big firm of ships' chandlers who had a lot of contracts with the Royal Navy. The things I saw!

Charlie was there in Berlin, a corporal in the London Rifles, when it was liberated. I don't often get upset but last Sunday morning I tuned in to Radio 4 by mistake and there was a special service from Westminster Abbey to commemorate the Battle of Britain. Some bigwig RAF man was talking about the night the blitz began in London, 7 September, 1940 – 'Black Saturday' – and I won't ever forget it.

So as RAF bigwig is speaking, I look out the window, and I could hear them all over again, the ack-ack guns, and see the barrage balloons, the screech of the air-raid sirens, smell burning in the streets. You'd never believe what we all went through in Hackney. Then they sang a hymn, and we heard Churchill's voice. Now, I voted Labour in the 1945 General Election and I was never a Churchill worshipper – not like some down the British Legion in Morning Lane. But when I heard that voice, no one could deny that man was a miracle: 'Now if the British Empire should survive for a thousand years, let them say this was their finest hour.' Can you think of one modern politician who could talk like that? Not on your life. I was crying that much I had to put my chocolate caramel in a piece of tissue.

When I look at people today I often wonder: What would you fight for? What would make you go on? What would you die for? 'We shall never surrender' − I reckon this lot would. I had a bit of a turn after that, very tearful, but then I had a nice piece of boiled gammon for my tea and two bottles of Guinness.

The next morning I woke feeling very fresh, read the *Daily Mirror* cover to cover in bed. There was a knock. So I gets up in my dressing-gown, peeps through the eye-hole, and opens the door. This tall, handsome young gentleman, reddy-fair hair, blue eyes, stands there with a clipboard. 'I'm from London Electricity,' he says 'and as you know we are all sharing suppliers for gas now so if you would like to sign this form.'

'I never sign forms straight off.'

'Madam, you must.'

'Give me the forms.'

'We must sign it now, madam.'

He's leaning forward. Well, perhaps I should. So I take his pen. 'No,' I says, 'bugger off − I ain't signing nothing till I've looked at it.'

He stepped further forward − 'Just sign the form, madam' − and I'm trying to close the door, and he wedges his foot on the door-ledge.

I stepped back, and round the side I picked up my old cast-iron fire-poker I keep there just in case. I opened the door − and took a mighty crack at his left foot.

'Owh, Owh, Owh!'

'Hop it, mate! − or you'll get another!'

I held the poker right up but he hobbled away like a right little coward.

I closed the door, had a big laugh, then poured myself a whisky in the kitchen and sat in the front room. My old tabby cat came meowing and sat on my lap. I said to her, 'We didn't go through the war for nothing, did we, Lilly?'

Old and New

The crowded 38 lunged to a halt at the bus-stop on the Balls Pond Road. I swayed and my ankle was tapped by a small brown polished lace-up brogue, which hovered as it tried to touch the floor.

'Sorry, love.'

'That's okay,' I said.

My hand was grasped by the small elderly owner of the shoe, who drew herself up to her full height of about five foot. Her round dark hat of Panama straw was askew. She adjusted it and smiled. The pastel-shaded flower decorations round the brim and sides, marigolds perhaps, wobbled away from the binding.

'These modern bus drivers is a curse,' she tutted.

She looked up like a rugby hooker as the scrum meshed round her. The doors opened and she held my arm.

'Thanks, love.'

She tugged and the force of her assumption drew me off the bus though I had not reached my stop. Her shopping bag – 'Hackney Recycles' – got caught between the legs of a large woman with a bright Jamaican scarf, who bent down and picked up two escaped tins of Sainsbury's baked beans. She handed me the bag: 'Lovely to see a man bein' good to his mother.' She beamed me an evangelical smile.

We found ourselves standing on the pavement.

'Which way?' I asked gallantly.

'You are lovely, that black woman was right. Don't get me wrong, no racism in me; I was an auxiliary nurse.'

She beckoned with her finger. I walked beside her with the heavy bag.

'My 'usband used to buy tools there.'

She pointed to 'Demetriou Zingas', its window piled high with saws, screwdrivers, chisels, plug spanners, tape measures, metal and cloth. My companion's coat was thickly-woven tweed, green and brown with highlighted flecks of brick red. The material was bobbled, the cuffs frayed, but the woman, and the old shop, side-by-side, looked natural and from another time. Next door the neon-lit COSTCUTTERS had 'Offers' plastered over the plate-glass front.

We crossed gingerly at the traffic lights and she pointed to pigeons settling on the roof of Hintons, plumbers' merchants. She told me about the houses and shops and the people who had owned them.

Marching towards us, fifty yards down the pavement, was a young woman in dark Lycra, sunglasses, white trainers, rucksack. At twenty yards, my friend jaywalked, the girl's arms pushed outwards. 'Be careful!' I said. The girl's elbow winged the old lady. The girl pushed on as the beat from her headphones insulated her against the public world.

'Young-uns!' We stopped outside a three-storey terraced house with net curtains and peeling cream paint on the woodwork. 'We're 'ere. You've done your good deed for the day.'

She held out her right hand and the sun sparked on her ruby ring. She toddled up the steps with her bag. I looked up the road, and the girl had crossed. When I turned back my new friend was inside, the door still open. The green paint on the walls in the hallway must have been fading for years.

Harry Slocombe's East End Return

Harry threw off the duvet, jumped up and looked out at a wet January Hackney morning, the grey canal bubbling past; he had agreed with Roz Aust, his analyst, he should get up early. 'What for?' He shivered; the central heating was broken. He lit a Camel, and lay down. 'Balls!' Ash fell on the cover. He went into the kitchenette and pressed down the greasy switch on the plastic kettle. 'Canal Side with a View' the estate agent had said. On the balcony the diesel-rich mist settled like sweat on his shaved head.

A retriever-looking puppy, its belly bloated and tight like a drum skin, was caught on the branch of a willow tree. 'Always a few after Christmas,' he muttered. Harry switched on the answerphone: 'Mistah Sylvester is veree pleased you haave taken the caisse of his missing dauughtah. He will contaact you sooon.' The line went dead. 'Sounds more like a threat.' He flicked the cigarette over the balcony.

'Positive thoughts in the morning, Harry; why is that so difficult for you?' Roz Aust had asked him at their last session. He picked up the reunion invitation card to 'Detective Inspector Slocombe.' It had been two years since he resigned. Across the marshes to Walthamstow the sky was grey; to the south-east a church spire poked between two high-rise blocks. 'There's nothing bleeding positive here, Roz, is there love.'

His large hand gripped his third mug of tea as he read the notes on seventeen-year-old Jasmine Sylvester. She was the daughter of Nicki Sylvester, Jamaican Import-Export specialist, six foot four, fourteen and a half stone, crocodile shoes, gold chains as thick as his fingers — not the sort of man to use the police.

Pretty girl, Harry thought as he shaved. Eau Sauvage stung his face — he threw away the Brut last week. He zipped up his black leather bomber jacket and rubbed his face: the skin was smooth for a smoker and drinker and his face had become thinner. He punched his stomach: thirteen and a half stone but he was training again at the gym. He stared at the mirror, rubbed his firm lips, and smiled.

His analyst had cropped hair, but he'd got over that. It was part of the deal; no threats to his pension, no inquiry, if he agreed to sort out his drinking. He kept her on after the money ran out from the police charity-fund grant.

He ran down the steps; the white 1967 Volvo was parked in the closest parking bay and started first time. 'Jasmine Sylvester, Jasmine Sylvester', he rolled her name on his tongue. He was on a search again, a hunt, a game, a race with gold at the end of the journey. 'Sam James, Hackney Auto Sports, Furlong Lane, E9.' His first contact. Sam's daughter, Hope, was the best friend of Jasmine Sylvester.

Harry parked in the debris-strewn yard, and walked slowly into the cavernous garage.

'Sam?' Harry shouted above the music, 'I'm Harry Slocombe, private investigator, working for Mr Sylvester.'

Sam turned off the CD player.

'Like classical music, Mr James?'

'Wagner's my man; that's the *Faust Overture*, one of his early bum-fluff works'.

'Very knowledgeable.'

'You think niggers only like jungle music?'

'Not at all, Mr James; I'm a jazz man myself.'

The tall supple Sam James put his head deeper into the engine compartment of a chrome-bumper red MGB.

'Mr Sylvester said you'd help me; his daughter has gone missing.'

'Mr Sylvester?' Sam picked up a plug spanner.

In the corner of the workshop a fierce shaved-head black guy dropped a wrench. Sam hit his head against the bonnet and gestured for Harry to follow. He led the way up a metal staircase to a bare storage room-cum-office.

'I don't see my daughter, we quarrel, she gone off.'

'Address?'

'Don't know, we quarrel.'

'Wonder if Mr Sylvester thinks his daughter's got something valuable of his, something he wants back?'

'You talkin' riddles.'

'Jasmine Sylvester, had a boyfriend, Winston, big boy, handsome, clever, worked for Mr Sylvester as a courier; he was being trained for management.'

'Girls have boyfriends, man, make the world go round.'

'And Jasmine and her boyfriend, Winston, they went off together?'

'Happens all the time.' Sam breathed heavily.

At the bottom of the stairs, trainers squeaked.

Harry looked out. Fast-food cartons littered the street's grimy gutter. He tried to look over the roofs to Hackney Marshes but chimneys blocked his view. His mother's aunts lived in Burma Road, his granddad was born in Bethnal Green, and Harry had started as a constable in Bow. Was there no escape? he thought. 'Mr Sylvester is a powerful man, Sam, if he doesn't get his possessions back.'

'Don't twist me up, man.'

'You want Mr Sylvester to question your daughter, use his own men, their kind of tactics?'

'So why's Mr Sylvester not here now, if he so keen?'

'Keeping a professional distance, Sam; may I call you Sam?'

Sam picked up a pen and scribbled down his daughter's address, 'I think she knows where Jasmine is but I don't want trouble for Hope.'

'Trouble, Sam?'

'Sylvester's gone crazy. Drugs, big time.'

'Grass?'

'Big deal!'

'Heroin. He wants to take over London — if he troubles Hope.'

Harry jerked open the door. 'Like listening to other people's conversations, son?' The cropped-haired man glared.

'Me worry 'bout Sam, having an ex-old bill sniffling round like a dog on heat.' He thrust his big face at Sam.

'Who told you that, son?'

'Me got ears everywhere, remember dat, Sam!'

'Got a car to work on, sonny?'

'Rasclat!' He slammed the door.

'If I need more information, shall we have a drink, a meal perhaps; the Dutch Pot, best Caribbean food in London?'

'Thought you a pie-and-mash man.' Sam held his head in his hands. 'Here's my number, keep it from Voodoo Face.'

'Until we meet again.'

Harry sat in the Volvo. He read Hope's address, '29 Vallance Road, Bethnal Green'. He sped off. 'Getting bigger all the time, if I get the H back to Sylvester, big money – and I need the money.'

Adrenalin pumped his genitals like a dose of oysters – Martha the Bondage Maid, who he'd seen for twenty years – though his wife never knew until the end. Martha made him safe, holding his body, his self, all he was, in one place, ordered, controlled. 'Talk to the images, talk to them, enter a dialogue?' Roz was keen on dialogues. But he wanted change, freedom, love.

He parked near Vallance Road. 'Funny to think the Krays were born here.'

Sam must have phoned his daughter and she let Harry in at once. Hope was tall, strong like a swimmer, her hair in ringlets. 'We need to talk, tell me about Jasmine.' Five minutes later she had told him nothing of use.

'Look outside,' Harry suggested.

On the corner, two black heavies slunk by a lamp-post.

115

'Don't worry, love, they're only checking I'm doing my job, they won't get involved; after all Mr Sylvester had his reputation to consider.'

She let go of the curtain and tears rolled down her cheeks.

'I'm frightened, Mr Slocombe. Jasmine Sylvester's my best friend, we're like sisters, such a stupid girl, going off with Winston like that, stealing Mr Sylvester's...' She was shaking.

Harry handed her a pen and a scrap of paper and she scribbled an address. 'I'll sort it, thanks. Bye — and keep safe.'

Harry drove up Bethnal Green Road and the drizzle reflected the tail lights of cars; in the shop windows there were gaudy displays of drinks, perfumes and magazines.

Winston wanted to get away from Sylvester, so he thought he would steal a kilo of heroin, and make a new life for him and Jasmine back home, in Jamaica.

'Back home' — they were born in Homerton Hospital! Harry didn't try to lose the red XJ6 that was following him.

At his apartment he kept the lights off, and looked out at the towpath. By the Anchor the two heavies glanced up at his place, and flicked their cans of lager into the canal. Harry yawned, had a cold shower, lay on his bed and picked up the phone: 'No, I want to talk to Mr Sylvester directly.'

'He's too busy,' a deep male voice said.

'Things have moved on. Get Mr Sylvester — we don't want the police involved in this new situation, do we?'

Silence.

'Mr Slocombe, Mr Sylvester here. You're not trying to threaten me, are you?'

'No games, Mr Sylvester. Two grand straight up. It's not just your daughter you want back, is it? I'll get the stuff back to you. And when I do, you leave Jasmine and Winston alone, okay; I've still got contacts in the police.'

'Of course, Mr Slocombe. Always knew I know I could trust an ex-Met. private dick.'

'I'll be in touch.'

Harry swilled black coffee round his mouth. 'I'll sort this out. No time for morality.'

A commotion outside. Only kids with white plastic bags. Glue sniffers. Girl and two boys, white as death, going onto the marshes for their evening fun. It would never end, the muddle, the mess. Only Martha understood, as her leather thighs straddled his body.

He cleaned up his flat and lay on his bed. He woke cold from a fitful sleep. 'What can I bloody do?' He phoned George Ormrod, now a detective sergeant with the Robbery Squad. Harry had trained him. They used to call George Cissy Hot Pants because his trousers were always pressed; it was rumoured he was a Baptist.

'George, it's Harry.'

He gave Harry information about Sylvester, and it was all bad – there wasn't anything Sylvester wouldn't do. 'If you can pass on anything about Sylvester, Harry; he's an evil bastard.'

'I'll try.' He put down the phone and lit a cigarette.

He looked up at the skylight in the ceiling which gave access to a fire escape that led to the other side of the building. He climbed up the stepladders, bellied over the roof to keep out of sight of the thugs on the towpath, and shinned down the other side.

The Volvo was parked in Digby Road. 'Start, my darling, start.' As he raced off, one of the heavies turned. 'Too late, bastards; maybe Sylvester will cut off your balls.'

He took a back route to Commercial Road then followed it east to the Isle of Dogs. Jasmine and Winston were living in an apartment on Narrow Street. He ran to the lifts, smelt the river, sixth floor, number 129, knocked. No one answered and he called through the letterbox: 'Jasmine? Your friend Hope James told me I would find you here. I'm Harry Slocombe, love; I'm here to sort things out.' Winston opened the door, and smiled, as if welcoming a guest to the party. He led the way into the living room.

'I hate Sylvester,' Winston shouted. 'Praise the Lord! I hate him, evil man, son of Satan.'

Harry stood back, open mouthed.

'Be happy, Mr Slocombe. Happy days!' Jasmine shook his arm, 'We're born again. Praise the Lord. Sylvester's not my real dad, he just lives with my mum, one of his women — and he took a fancy to me too, many times — the Lord will punish him, Praise the Lord.'

'Hallelujah, Hallelujah!' Winston clapped his hands.

Harry blinked. 'I'm very happy for you both, naturally, but there is one small problem.'

'The heroin, Mr Slocombe, the devil's friend.' Winston smiled more broadly.

'Mr Sylvester wants his property back.'

'Never!' Winston shot up a Black Panther clenched fist.

'You destroyed it, you born again, dead again, little twit...'

'We hide it,' he said.

Harry sat down while Jasmine and Winston looked at the river, their arms round each other. Harry stared at them.

'All right kids, how far are you prepared to go? Will you testify against Sylvester?'

'Testify, testify!' they cheered.

'Oh my God,' Harry said.

They sat on either side of Harry. Jasmine held his hand, tenderly, 'We're not mad, Mr Slocombe; of course we are afraid to give evidence; Sylvester will try to kill us, but Winston's brother died from heroin last month, so the Lord will protect us when we are in court — we're going to do it, all the way.' Her bright eyes gazed into his. For a moment he felt free — Martha's handcuffs unlocked.

Winston stood, 'The Lord will protect us.'

It's only money, Harry sighed, and watched two thousand pounds burning in front of his eyes.

'All right kids, if you really want to, I know a police detective who will make sure you're protected.' He looked round the room. 'Put that chest of drawers across the door, and the wardrobe against the window – do it, now!'

He used his mobile: 'George, it's Harry. I've found Sylvester's heroin, and the two kids will make a statement – they've found salvation.'

'Say that again.'

'I've not been drinking, they had a conversion experience. No, George, they've not changed to Virgin, they're born again. I'll explain later. Get down here, now – bring a team, an armed unit; I mean that.' He rubbed his head and turned: 'He's on his way, kids. Make us a cup of tea will you, love?'

An hour later George Ormrod arrived with two detectives, handguns bulging under their jackets. In the kitchen, Harry discussed the case with them.

Then he went into the living room: 'I'll leave you to it. Bye Hope, bye Winston.'

Harry drove down the East India Dock Road, and parked. He opened the boot. If they can do it, so can I, he thought. He took out a Jiffy bag and walked across the gangplanks to the river. He gave his favourite handcuffs a kiss, put them back in the bag and flung it into the Thames.

'Goodbye, Martha.'

When Jasmine looked into his eyes he knew he could change. He sat on the muddy riverbank, closed his eyes and saw his handcuffs travelling past Millwall towards the open sea.

Lancashire Pudding

As I dozed, it sounded like my mother's voice from the radio, bringing her Lancashire tales into the Surrey world of my childhood.

At Sunday lunch she would tell stories about Grandma Piggott, who pickled herrings, and put snow in the pancakes. When 'Gentlemen of the Road' called at Carlton House they would always leave with their bellies full. Yes, it could have been my mother's voice: I imagined a landscape of belonging, far from London. I wanted to return to those slow-age days when Time did not shake beneath your feet and I could picnic in the Vale of Bowland. I stretched. It was Sunday and friends were coming.

I heard my mother's voice from the kitchen: 'With beef make sure it's Lancashire pudding'.

The Sculptor's Party

London plane trees shook off their leaves. Through the studio's translucent blind the patterns of stripped branches swerved over the floor and Laura made faces in front of the Victorian cheval mirror.

'Getting on?' the sculptor called from upstairs.

'Almost done,' she shouted above the sound of Pink Floyd's new double album, *Another Brick in the Wall*.

He stood at the door: 'Thought you would have finished.'

'Almost.' She pulled on her short black velvet dress, and touched one of her paintings, which were propped like vertical dominoes by the window. She heard her mother laughing at them.

'I'll hold the stepladders,' Nick said.

'Bet you will. No fanks.'

Her teeth chattered; she put on the Fair-Isle jumper, a Christmas present from her social worker: *Least she's not coming tonight, the way she looks at Nick, not letting him know straight, swishing her arse, flicking her hair. She ain't his type anyway.* Nick walked out but she heard him in her head — *Come on Laura, this is for you, get cracking* — which was better than some of the other voices. Just because he was an artist she didn't see why he always liked paint on his T-shirts. She carried painting 'No 6' and hung it on the nail marked '6'. Half an hour later most of her paintings were in place.

In the basement kitchen she made a strong mug of tea, stirred in two spoonfuls of sugar, and went in to the junk room where she listened in the dark. The open fire hissed. She stacked on more wood, then rolled up her sleeve: 'One, two, three — like sergeant's stripes.' The last cut was raised and purple. Her soldier ex-boyfriend had explained Army ranks by drawing them on her belly with a felt pen; he joined the Parachute Regiment and she didn't see him again.

The music stopped. Another voice: 'What an evening, it'll be fine / Life is lovely, life is mine, / Life is full of bubbly wine / This is 1979.' Nick sang nonsense songs when he was happy and her fingers danced over the slashes on her arm. He was nice looking but cocky; she wasn't going to just because he'd split with his girlfriend. The flames shaped scenes from life in the Bermondsey flat: mother, brother, half brother, 'uncles' – their faces blocked the chimney. Tobacco and cigarette paper crumbled as she squeezed. *Snotty bitch-boss from Social Services kept sending people to see we wasn't screwing.* 'Ha naw braun coww.' She watched her lips in the cracked wall mirror and practised speaking like Nick. She lived here because he rented rooms and John and Jenny, the couple on the third floor, knew her social worker.

Above her, tables and chairs scraped as Nick arranged the studio. He had made the maquettes for Pink Floyd's *Brick in the Wall* Tour and one of the band was coming tonight. The mirror made rude faces as she put on mascara, and then Nick appeared, telling her to hurry up, as if they were going on a date.

'Fuckin' 'ell, is that the time?' Saws, hanging from the beams, vibrated. She brushed her long brown wiry hair, and adjusted her low cream top. She unlocked the door. 'Hello,' she said. Nick stood there in black jeans and a crumpled white silk shirt.

'You look great,' he said.

'Not bad yourself, pity 'bout the shoes.' She stared at his off-white Green Flash.

'Bourgeois.'

'Scruffy git. Don't yer know what an iron is?'

The front doorbell rang.

'Thanks for inviting me,' the soft female voice said as Nick opened the door.

Fucking shit. Laura bit the back of her hand as Suzie Dyson, Laura's social worker, kissed Nick on both cheeks. Suzie turned: 'It's great you've done all this,' and her long radiant blonde hair touched Laura's cheek.

'Fanks.' Laura coughed. *She smells like a fuckin' flower shop.* Laura watched as Nick talked to Suzie about Laura's drawings and she replied all la-di-da. 'Notice the fine details in the pattern,' Nick said and Suzie added, 'I like how the figures change colour in sequence.' *Bollocks.* Laura mimicked retching. *Don't fink you're going to get him, tart.*

'You're interested in art?' Nick asked Suzie.

'My father is an architect; he taught me how to look at things.'

Like Nick's crotch.

The studio soon filled up with guests and the Prosecco fizzed.

'The local Indian restaurant is bringing food later,' Nick said as he turned up Pink Floyd.

Laura poured wine for Suzie and managed to spit in the glass. Family voices shouted in her head and the scars throbbed on her arm. Within an hour most of the guests had arrived. An hour later the food came. Laura pretended to eat but didn't because she knew Indians put cats in the curry.

'I like the one where the girls look like sexy Daleks,' a tall dark man said to Laura, an ankh dangling from his open blue psychedelic shirt.

'Yours for fifty quid, mate.'

'You were miles away. I'm Paul, a roadie with the Floyd.'

'Pleased to meet yer,' she said as she weighed him up; she glanced at a glossy man in the other corner of the studio. 'Is that...?'

'Yeah.'

Nick came over and told her she had sold three paintings.

'If this carries on I'll be buying the fuckin' studio off you. Cheers.'

Suzie was being chatted up by someone in a suede jacket and cowboy boots. *Stick wiv im, love, as he's just right for an old scrubber like you.*

Laura ran down to the kitchen, turned the cold tap to full and the rush took away the voices in her head. She gulped a glass of water and picked up her fizzy-wine glass. '50, 100, 200', she counted the bubbles as they rose. She went into the basement and the top hinge juddered as the door shut. She held the glass close to her mouth and licked the good dream bubbles.

Nick came in. 'You're shivering,' he said, put his black elephant-cord jacket round her shoulders, and collected a few of his prints. They went into the kitchen.

'Cheers.' She sipped and gave him the glass. 'Thanks for everything. What clubs do yer like, then?'

'Dingwalls is my favourite.'

'I'll treat yer with my earnings.'

'You keep your money.'

He pecked her on the cheek and went upstairs with his prints.

Her flesh tingled. *Still so much to learn about art.* Footsteps were loud on the stripped wooden stairs as guests went up to the top floor, and the basement door hinges stuttered as she slipped into the dark room. Ashes smouldered in the fireplace. *They're all laughin' at yer, Laura, with your la-di-da ways. And you know what Nick wants.* 'Get lost!' Laura screamed at her mother's voice.

She tripped over a canvas, her glass slipped as wine spilt – the bulb exploded and glass splintered across the floor. She blocked her ears against the noise from upstairs. *Bet they're like that all the time, party-to-party, never alone in a basement.* She put on the main light and reapplied her makeup.

She listened: their world was far away now but she forced herself, smiled to the mirror, and went to the top floor. Suzie and Nick were joking together at the far end and as Suzie reached behind for a drink her cheek touched his face. *Slag.* Laura danced with Paul the roadie, who said he would take her to a gig next week, Laura said maybe, and people chatted with her and praised her work until it was the end of the party.

She touched each of her paintings but they didn't belong to her anymore. She tiptoed to the bottom of the stairs and sat down. The music had stopped but Suzie hadn't left and Laura could hear them clearly. Suzie said, 'I'm following an R D Laing theme for my PhD thesis about the falseness of labels in diagnosing schizophrenia. It's post-Laing, you know, but he led the way.'

'I read *Knots*,' Nick said.

'You've helped Laura so much. Art therapy is so underrated; have you read John Henzell's recent article by any chance?'

'Perhaps you could lend it to me? Laura is coming along well, just needs a boyfriend.'

She heard Nick say to Suzie, 'I don't think you've seen all the show. My maquettes are in the corner.'

'Yes please.'

Laura went to the kitchen to make tea; she gripped the mug so tight that her palms turned red. The white kitchen was a waiting room and soon the nurse would say '*Come in and see the psychiatrist now and he'll give you more drugs to keep you tame*'. She crept up to the studio, took *Another Brick in the Wall* back to the basement and put it on. She knelt down and stoked the fire. Her mother's angry face looked out from the flames. Tears wet her fingers and she lay down on the hard floor: the silence locked her out. A little later she sat up as the front door opened.

'Thanks for a lovely evening,' Suzie said.

A pause, perhaps a few pecks on the cheek?

'Bye,' Nick said, 'thanks for coming.'
He came down to the basement: 'You okay?'
'Better now.'
'Want to go to Dingwalls next week?'
'If yer wear proper shoes.'
'Bourgeois.'
'Scruffy git.'